Carníval

Carnível
a Scream In High Park reader

edited by Peter McPhee

INSOMNIAC PRESS

Compilation copyright © 1996 Peter McPhee
Copyright of the writers' works remain with the authors

All rights reserved. No part of this publication may be reproduced, stored in a retrieval system or transmitted, in any form or by any means, without the prior written permission of the publisher or, in case of photocopying or other reprographic copying, a licence from CANCOPY (Canadian Copyright Licensing Agency), 6 Adelaide St. E., Suite 900, Toronto, Ontario, Canada, M5C 1H6.

Edited by Peter McPhee
Copy edited by Lloyd Davis, Gayle Irwin, damian lopes, Mike O'Connor,
        Liz Thorpe, Darren Wershler-Henry, Alana Wilcox
Designed by Mike O'Connor

Canadian Cataloguing in Publication Data

Main entry under title:

Carnival: a Scream in High Park reader

Stories and poems from the writers who performed at the Scream in High Park in its first 3 years.
ISBN 1-895837-38-3

1. Short stories, Canadian (English) .* 2. Canadian fiction (English) - 20th century.* 3. Canadian poetry (English) - 20th century.* I. Scream in High Park (Toronto, Ont.). II. McPhee, Peter, 1964-   .

PS8233.C37 1996   C810.8'054   C96-930387-4
PR9194.4.C37 1996

Printed and bound in Canada

Insomniac Press
378 Delaware Ave.
Toronto, Ontario, Canada, M6H 2T8

Table of contents

Introduction		xi
1995		**1**
Nicole Brossard	Matter Harmonious Still Maneuvering	3
Gerry Shikatani	Mezquita	8
	Who Notes: A Particular Pronoun, A	
	Responsibility	10
Claire Harris	Jane In Summer	11
	Kay In Summer	13
Dannabang Kuwabong	The Guns Of Kigali Are Silent	15
Wendy Agnew	How To Make Love To An Angel	19
	from The Lillian Lectures	21
Matthew Remski	*from* dying for veronica	24
Patricia Seaman	*from* Super Nevada	27
Stuart Ross	Around The Building	30
	Velvet Curtains	32
Eileen O'Toole	Florist	33
	Sam's	34
Jaymz Bee	Clint East Woody Allen Alda	35
André Alexis	Pierrot	36
Elise Levine	True Romance	39
	Untitled, artist's collection	40
	This Is It	41
John Barlow	The Happy Idea	42
1994		**47**
Bill Kennedy	*from* Apostrophe	49
Nancy Bullis	Linseed Oil	54
Death Waits	Breaking Skin	57
	Goldfish Loves Wolf	58
Lise Downe	Déjà Déjà Vu	60
	Weather I	61
Rafael Barreto-Rivera	*from* Shredded What: a Whitman Serial	63
M. Nourbese Philip	Discourse On The Logic Of Language	67
Nino Ricci	*from* I am Salman Rushdie	71
Karen Mac Cormack	Some Miles Asunder	74
Al Purdy	At the Quinte Hotel	79
	My Grandfather's Country	81

Susan Musgrave	Out Of Time	84
	Arctic Poppies	85
	Water Music	87
	Holy Ground	88
Mac McArthur	We Sat In Open Fields	89
Nancy Dembowski	Mirror Writing	93
	Borders	94
	Ghosts	96
Steve McCaffery	Novel 39	98
	from Teachable Texts	99
	K As In Sleep	101
Sonja Mills	I Am So Fat	102
Leon Rooke	Sweethearts	104
Stan Rogal	Personations 21	107
	Dark Horses	109
Tricia Postle	Today I'm Going To Be A Man	111
	Commentary	114
Clifton Joseph	(I Remember) Back Home	115
R.M. Vaughan	Requiem from a Heady Height	117

1993   **123**

Yves Troendle	Dead Givaway (re: Robert Rauschenberg)	125
Adeena Karasick	Floruit Retinue	128
Christopher Dewdney	The Clouds	132
	The Fossil Forest of Axel Heiberg	133
	Vigilance	134
Roo Borson	Summer Cloud	135
	The Limits Of Knowledge, Tilton School, New Hampshire	136
Steven Heighton	Nakunaru	137
	The Ecstasy of Skeptics	139
Peter McPhee	Why The Stegosaurus Is My Favourite Dinosaur	140
Barbara Gowdy	Resurrection (1969)	144
michael holmes	*from* 21 Hotels	149
Christian Bök	*from* Crystallization	152
Christine Slater	*from* The Small Matter Of Getting There	155
Paul Dutton	Kit-Talk	159
	Shy Thought	160
	Bark	161

Lea Harper	Weekend Indians	162
	Birth	165
Sky Gilbert	Why This Poem Is Not Anything	
	Like Broccoli	167
	Breakfast In Key West	170
Lynn Crosbie	Pearl	171
David Donnell	What's So Easy About 17?	174
bill bissett	i was driving in 2 hundrid mile hous	
	in th karibu northern bc	177
	who has seen th defisit	178
	let th watr sit 4 a day n th	
	chloreen evaporates	179
Biographies		181
Acknowledgements		189

Part of the proceeds from the sale of this book will go to Frontier College.

Frontier College is a national non-profit literacy organization, which recruits and trains volunteers to tutor children, teens and adults who want to improve their reading and writing.

Frontier College was founded by students at Queen's University in 1899. Today, it works from university campus sites in every part of Canada.

The mission of Frontier College is to organize Canadians to fight poverty and to work for social justice by teaching people to read and write.

To the audience

Volunteers

All the work that makes the Scream possible is contributed on a voluntary basis. Whether collecting donations, making phone calls or putting up posters, we would like to thank the following for their selfless dedication:

Mike Barnard, Hazel Bice, John Boyle, Stephen Cain, Natalee Caple, Fides Coloma, Bonnie Halvorson, Troy and Christie Harkin, Gayle Irwin, Mike Jest, Bill Kennedy, Stefan Lehmann, damian lopes, Tom MacKay, Henry Martinuk, Patrick McPhee, Jay MillAr, Brian Panhuyzen, Lora Patton, Dennison Smith, Clive Thompson, Helen Tsiriotakis, Darren Wershler-Henry, Alana Wilcox.

Friends

The Scream In High Park would like to thank the following for their support and contributions:

Keith Anderson and everyone at Canadian Stage Company, Stan Bevington, Nicky Drumbolis, letters bookshop, the Coach House Press printers, Harold Bulmanis, Lorraine Filyer and the Literature Department at the Ontario Arts Council, Jane Larimer, the Metropolitan Toronto Movement for Literacy, Beth Learn, Joy Learn, John and Nancy McPhee, Tim Neesam, Pat Profiti and the staff of Toronto Parks and Recreation, Aaron Tahm, Printcom, Eddy Yanofsky, Nick Power, University of Toronto Bookstore, Mike O'Connor, Marlene Warnick, Alex Terrier, Quality Hotel, Adita Petrauskaite, Sandra Drzewiecki, the League of Canadian Poets, Diane Alley, Pam Robenson, Coach House Press Publishing, Ray Cronin, Goose Lane Editions, Sean Power, Selina Martin, Sam Hiyate, Katy Chan, Amanda Huggins, Katherine Jevons, University of Toronto Writer's Workshop, Saul Jonas, Ludwig Zeller, Kelly Hechler, McClelland & Stewart, Gutter Press, and John Miller who was a catalyst in the evolution of this collection.

We gratefully acknowledge the UofT Bookstore, Bob Miller Book Room and Canadian Stage for being with us from the beginning. The Scream receives financial assistance from the Ontario Arts Council, the Canada Council Reading Programme and the League of Canadian Poets through the Metropolitan Toronto Department of Cultural Affairs.

Introduction

As our starting point we have contemporary reality, the living people who occupy it together with their opinions. From this vantage point, from this contemporary reality with its diversity of speech and voice, there comes about a new orientation in the world and in time through personal experience and investigation.

— *M.M. Bakhtin*

At 6 p.m., at Pearson International Airport, the sky is overcast, the temperature steady at 21 degrees. The humidity registers at 81 percent. The barometric pressure is at 101.1 kilopascals and falling slowly. Variable cloudiness this evening, with a low of 17 degrees. Clearing towards midnight.

— *Environment Canada Forecast, July 18, 1993*

We wanted a celebration of poetry and storytelling. We wanted to be lost for an evening on a midway of voice. Voice like caramel, sticking to our fingers. Voice of adrenaline, of inspiration. Exhilarating, head spinning. We wanted carnival. And where could our Toronto raised image of carnival dance with those raised in Trinidad, New Orleans or Markinch, Saskatchewan? Scream In High Park became an eclectic meeting of background, viewpoint, and writing style. A momentary blend of voices forming a single, unrepeatable expression of the possible. The carny wasn't asking us to buy, just to come in and discover...

In the winter of 1993, Matthew Remski, a 21-year-old poet, small press publisher and community radio broadcaster, was organizing a reading. He had learned that the Shakespearean stage, at the site of Canadian Stage's annual summer production Dream In High Park, would not be used on

Monday nights. He was going to hold an outdoor poetry festival. (I won't trouble you with the story of how he chose a name except to say, he was inspired.) The rest of us thought a festival was a great idea and offered many suggestions — but very little help. He drew on and then enhanced our sense of community.

By the first week of July, preparations were complete. Sixteen writers would read from their work (and be paid for it). Matthew put up posters. He also put up most of the money. It hadn't rained in weeks.

It rained the night before the first Scream In High Park. It poured. I lay awake listening to it. Matthew, only a few blocks away and likely calling the Environment Canada hot line every fifteen minutes; trying to prepare for the uncontrollable.

It rained off and on throughout the morning of July 19 and only started to clear in the afternoon. We had hoped people would come early with picnics. At 5:30, with a television crew broadcasting live from site, there were seven people on the hill which forms the amphitheatre. We knew six of them. The tv producer was not impressed. However, at 7 o'clock we had an audience of 450. And by the end of the night we knew it would happen again. (Matthew was already talking about August. He needed sleep.)

The following winter, I was late for a meeting at which Matthew confirmed his imminent dispatch to Prague. By the time I arrived, I had the artistic director's job. But I was not alone. Scream In High Park runs on the time and energy donated by a team of volunteers who share a belief in the celebration of poetry. Indeed, many of the writers included in these pages have either been involved from the beginning, or have returned to help in whatever way they can, whether by contacting other writers or by collecting donations on the hill. There are three names that do not appear in the table of contents that deserve mention since they have made integral contributions to all three festivals: Tom MacKay, stage manager; Darren Wershler-Henry, volunteer coordinator and general adviser; and Alana Wilcox, who did everything from making phone calls to copy editing this collection. Together, we have watched the Scream's audience grow to more than 1,200 people.

And now we've gone and put it in a book. It was never our intention to simply document what was read, nor to compile the definitive work of each contributor. *Carnival* is an attempt to capture some of the magic that is Scream In High Park, cast it in a slightly different direction, and create a new spell. It listens to voices that have gathered in the summer air and asks how they will interact when you, the reader, can choose how to free them from the page.

When programming Scream In High Park, we tend to encourage new writing, work in progress, and pure experimentation (though we are not above pure entertainment). Each year, we hope to present a fresh combination of imagery, idea and sound. We have a five-year moratorium on repeat performers. We try to remember our history while looking to our future. Some of the writers we select are pioneers of possibility when it comes to style and language. Others see tradition through unique eyes. Some you will know. Others are emerging, often after years of developing their craft. Many have opposing views, but a brief glimpse at their biographies reveals a shared willingness to promote expression by expanding to other art forms: film, video, music, theatre, and visual art.

When making the selections for this collection, I asked each writer what they would read if the Scream were held today. This approach yielded an abundance of new work, and many of the pieces here are previously unpublished. Of course, I made a few requests and these, too, produced some surprises. Al Purdy had recently rewritten *My Grandfather's Country*. The version included in *Carnival* contains a new third verse. Similarly we have included a new version of Christopher Dewdney's *The Fossil Forest of Axel Heiberg*.

Carnival echoes the time constraints of the Scream in that it is hardest on the prose writers. Nino Ricci confessed to the audience that as he had 12 minutes to read he thought he might only have to write for 12 minutes, and then added that he had been wrong. He has allowed us to excerpt the story he read in 1994, which is still in progress. Other fiction writers dealt with the time constraints in different ways: Leon Rooke contributes the short story he read on the night, Elise Levine sends us postcard fiction, André Alexis combines criticism and fiction, and Barbara Gowdy, Patricia Seaman and Christine Slater contribute excerpts from novels.

I have enjoyed every minute of each Scream In High Park and, while piecing *Carnival* together, I tried to include the elements which have made it such a unique event: the casual atmosphere and outdoor setting; the extraordinary writers; the humour and poignancy of the readings; the voices; the celebration; the summer night air. I will never forget reading at the first Scream. The sun had just set and the silhouettes of the people at the top of the hill were blending into the sky, mixing with my voice, and approaching infinity. I think one's sense of place becomes distorted.

xiv Carnival

In our current cultural climate there is something unreal about listening to poetry in a park, surrounded by the country's largest city (though the act is natural enough and the writing well grounded). At Scream In High Park we are everywhere at once. A place only magic can take us. We arrive, hear the voices and wonder if this is how carnival sounds.

Peter McPhee
Artistic Director
Scream In High Park

SCREAM IN HIGH PARK
a carnival of the spoken word
July 17, 1995

7:00 pm
Wendy Agnew *&* Matthew Remski
Patricia Seaman *&* André Alexis

8:00 pm
Ahdri Zhina Mandiela *&* Gerry Shikatani
Nicole Brossard *&* Dannabang Kuwabong

9:00 pm
Claire Harris *&* Stuart Ross
Elise Levine *&* Jaymz Bee

10:00 pm
Dionne Brand *&* John Barlow
Eileen O'Toole *&* Black Katt

Location: On the set of the Canadian Stage Company's Dream in High Park (East of the Grenadier Restaurant).

Suggested Donation $5.00. Bring a picnic, a blanket, cushions, and a friend.
Host: Peter McPhee   phone: (416) 532-6948   e-mail: bo253@torfree.net   Rain date: July 24

MONDAY, JULY 17, 1995
ATTENDANCE: 1,200

Nicole Brossard

MATTER HARMONIOUS STILL MANEUVERING

I presume that day breaks in more than one place and because this thought comes to me in the midst of reality and its unnameable poses I turn, bearing witness to the mobility of time and languages, to the thought that nothing is either too slow, or too fleeting for the universe

I know that all has not been said because my body has settled into this thought with a certain happiness and because amid the inexplicable jolt which makes of words a passage, running water and so much thirst, I can, by linking vowels and the backside of thoughts, eyes narrowed in fascination, approach death and its opposite

4 Carnival

at this late hour when the suppleness of the gaze is at its peak and life turns and turns again between the blue and astonishing law of lighted cities, at this late hour when words grip the chest as they do in operas and images await the flickering line of fever and of the future, my eyes bent so low upon humanity wonder from the very root of eyes of desire

all has not been said because I know that in languages I love radically, the rose shells of meaning, the assiduous structures which graft ecstasies and torrential matter in the midst of the voice and its behaviour, secret matter, rounder matter, matter like your sighs and still other liquids today I know that the bluest structure of the sea draws near to our cells and to untouchable suffering the way life circles three times around our childhood without ever really touching it because we are close to reality and matter cannot fall without warning us, without leaving us there, our skin hesitating between philosophies and the dawn, half and forever in torment, in the vast complication of beauty

all has not been said since the body is punctual and there remain red versions, and rare gestures, an incredible synchrony of the senses where thought, always positioned well for alliance, takes care to reconstitute in the mind symmetrically and sonorously sometimes even prior to ourselves the scenes and the beautiful portraits we love to dream for there are traits which attract us if only for an instant so as to die close to happiness hollowing out the universe with our shoulders and all the little imaginary lips which work mercilessly, lest we miss life, to invent the world and the cosmos for us very permanently like the absolute proportion of our hands when they caress so indistinctly with voice and palm that human body which has breasts

6 Carnival

at this late hour I know that life can confirm silence, can set fire to approvals, trace circular tears and engender dust and I like it this way for I've learned between July and October to look at all the fires, to steep myself in the strong smell of nudity, especially in the splendour of mauves, of facades and of the strange sonnets which gesticulate in language as we do in the night, dreaming so as not to die voiceless

all has not been said and I lunge forward my skin charged with cyprin* and echo because I long for a physical and thinking smile, inseparable from a nature long of breath; so when I look at stable objects and time turns upside down in my chest, splits open thought, elucidates death in a single leap, I know that all has not been said because my chest is tight

---

* Cyprin: female sexual secretion. English word coined by Susanne de Lotbinière-Harwood in her translation of Brossard's *Sous la langue*. (*Sous la langue/Under Tongue*, l'Essentielle, éditrices, 1987.)

at this late hour when memory is afraid of its leaps and the nerves in the midst of desire are overwhelmed with responses, I know that all has not been said, I know that light when it fractures shadow revives my respect for shadow and for light, I know that overflowing into the air of energy, the life that is mine engages me far away to breathe up close into my hand the long images of necessity and, of feeling, the beautiful breaches on the ground of dreaming and of identity,

at this late hour when naming is still a function of dreaming and of hope, when poetry separates dawn and the great rays of day and when many times over women will walk away — invisible and carnal — in the stories, I know that all has not been said because between urbane conversation and tradition it is cold in vertigo and sometimes in the volatile matter of tears a strange sweat of truth settles in as if life could touch its metaphors

Translated from the French by Lise Weil

Gerry Shikatani

MEZQUITA

CORDOBA

The wooden benches covered in dust
what is formed in the arch
the curve of the mosaic jewel
pocks of light, reflect upon, dust formed and covered
   swept up by the woman, a pushbroom quietly
on the marble floors in the morning — swish-swish
or a workman's power saw, restoration of site — sywz-sywz!

She is wandering, map in hand, description
in hand, the footsteps and there's a wooden bench
flying up towards an arch — that one there,

tracing spirit she moves not, but is dancer
more than just slave to those words, but by
the guidance of light, as it ciphers
the dark.

Forests of pillars and arches, the air
remains cool light changing its
habit with window miraculous, superb, nifty or
'Let's pray; Let Us Pray' it describes the space by which
it's confined: or it's also a postcard you bought it,
I bought one and she

walks in this direction of sound, steers
away now from the black metal barriers
which prison the dark alcoves
with their paintings and secret worship, secret hues (prayer
                              such beautiful chance)

     and a mumble is poetry, nonsense, speaking
     in tongues, leafing through; and by the doctor/therapist, kind
                    of a 'Sir Michelin'

she is told to lose the self by the trace of a path
sketched by details
: numbers, colours,
the codices of
history (in fact)
buy the complete kit, paint
by number, take a package
winter vacation
to wooden benches covered in dust, the Islamic,
the Mudejar, discover other cultures
and use no erasers;

a broom.

10 *Carnival*

Who Notes: A Particular Pronoun, A Responsibility

1. Inside

She walks slowly now heading to exit, that same entrance, portal of light
to grove described by the walls of the cathedral. Exit, but as if expecting
to be stopped, stopped in her path, a tap on her shoulder, a clearing of
the throat from the rear, or perhaps, a new thing remembered an excuse
like a painting she would of necessity turn round.
A catch, a run in the stocking.

2. Outside

(for in the break of speech of shifted dissonance) She is now there in the
sunlight, warming her cold fingers, gripping her books. The tower rises to
the right, the east of her. Almost faith in the archaeology of things, of
detail, (the shaking mysterious leaves) in the leaps of time, and thus to
surrender to the chain. The chain of light pulls with gentle despair, a
persuasion toward the rising. East of her, the sun is relentless, unstop-
pable, the cathedral tower to admire. The chain of the light.

3. Nether

Now unfolding her composite map and guide to this place into her
shoulder bag, she is taking gradual steps backwards very slowly — it is a
ridiculous scene: self-absorptive and contrived. The advancement is
quick, the pace quickens more (head races) leaning forward such
advance, yet stepping quickly backwards in blind. Now blind, running
sprint, the movement a dance like gentle persuaded fragments seemingly
seamless, taken from narration. In the forest of pillars, the hundreds of
pillars of, the jasmine and marble Mezquita, twirling absolute about her
the chain in a dervish way. In the archaeology of things she is thinking a
handwriting illegible, erased in places, she is surrendering to a faith in
things, almost not there.

A tap on the shoulder is all that remains to succeed. Does one continue
to the portal? Advance still backwards yet more?

Claire Harris

JANE IN SUMMER

She sits on rocks above the bay   so still that were it not
        for the wind in her hair   or her blouse in its yellow
        silk blooming
She might be a figure carved from twisted pine   from
        summer   curve of her back and arm growing from the curve
        of land
At this distance Barcelona suits her   a certain grace
        black hair   pale forehead
Yet you would be better to think her a room rising
        out of ruins   a room put together stone by stone
Stones unfamiliar to each other yet holding together
        with delicacy   despite cracks and patches

A stranger passing by at dusk   looking up in softened light
        might catch a glimpse   shadowy elegances
From consonants of chandelier and red velvet chair might
        construct a language   a fable   might imagine skeins of wool
        tapestry
And a woman graceful in summer glow waiting behind leafed
        wrought iron bars
If drawn to rescue he knocked on the door it would open on
        a warm prairie room   fire burning low   prim French provincial
        suite   dried flowers near the hearth   a table laid for two
        the air expectant
But no woman there   nothing but an empty room listening
        for someone else to come along the path   someone known

12 Carnival

Now each summer shaking off her year   its ruins   she comes
    to Spain   finds a new place to stitch and unstitch dreams
Summer after summer passes in an illusion of action   of vivid
    life   rehearsing her stories   and winter
And always   like an after-image or a ghost the first Adam
    secret inviolate moment   the love around which her life
    still swirls
Imagine then the stranger hesitating on her threshold
    conscious in the stones indifference   retracing his steps
    down paths of rosemary
Should he pause he might hear clear and distant   the voice
    of that room piping as in a darkening wood

KAY IN SUMMER

Someone   waiting in the lobby of a Hotel Imperial   amid
    the spaciousness   tourists   and peeling gold leaf
    might see it all as too hesitant for truth
Might think   for a moment   about the art in scattering
    too solidly carved tables   crowding too many dreams
    before dim victorian sofas
Might remember certain high-backed chairs   or a woman
    that could lend a touch of veracity to this place
From this   might wonder if truth is possible   if always
    and everywhere there is the notion   stage
    as true of a bed as of a lobby

Imagine now   Kay   as she steps through glass doors   and
    someone who glancing up   sees her suggest everything
    is possible   no   is probable in this place
Someone   who can tell from the easy music of her walk
    how decades and sophistication have slipped from her
    without a rustle
How she has stepped into these brighter softer eyes
    into this clear joyous laughter with out memory
Such a man now   iron-grey and ramrod   may welcome years
    hovering about her bare feet   scent of prairies
    songs of experience and struggle
May insist only on allegory: glitter and glass slippers
    smile on a killer toy

From the roof garden   opposite   our old old man ungentle
    in this summer night   gestures furiously   slashes
    at his wheelchair   a daughter burdened with wet sheets
    hurries to hang them
Then kneels before the old one to rub his hands between
    her own   until he smiles
I turn away from this   worrying its meaning   its small
    beauties   tiny hungers and comforts   how like
    an electric charge   the attentions of One

14 Carnival

They step together into the leafy romantic air   and
    Las Ramblas   Kay   jaunty as hell   her summer affairs
    the sloe burning flame that makes autumn bearable
That perfumes her air as she moves towards the grave
    its slow   inexorable stages
Jane   flat in her deck chair   calls to me...She didn't
    come to Barcelona for love   love is hard   one wants
    something softer   only a little pain   a little grace
    and limited fallout...

On our last evening I search for the word that is resolution
    to her story   but she dances down stone streets
    shimmies in tavernas   spins in the dim light
    and that spurious lobby
Perhaps more allegory   perhaps someone watching closely
    will see her catch her lower lip between bruising teeth
    on the stroke of midnight
Now high above the city we stand on that terrace
    I am saying   Look   look where we are   the rotting stone
    the ragged haze from a thousand years of intention
    the avenue   those trees
Listen   she says   listen to bells carve the hours

Dannabang Kuwabong

THE GUNS OF KIGALI ARE SILENT

The guns of Rwanda are silent.

the hunting and the laughter are gone
the thousand hills lie prostrate in gall
scarred by searing screams not lava streams
Oh! my voiceless land, Oh! my voiceless home!
let me rise with quiet haste of morning mist
and echo this bitterness of our desolation
I the sole taster of these saltless tears
gathered to chronicle your severed members
and the sirens of souls in pandemonium

for the guns of Rwanda lie silent.
The guns of Kigali are silent.

I sneak around the spokes of pain
I who have seen my weltering hopes
singed with the brushfires of spite
my faith creamed in craters of power
among these smoking Gisenyi volcanoes
but how do I refuse these sermons of pain
and the tired tongues of silent stares
my voice these tattered tear drops
of squatting skulls below the hills
searching for necks in battle dust

when guns of Kigali lie silent.
The guns of Butare are silent.

16 Carnival

so among the sticky grass of Rutuga
I rise with the smell of misty blood
wiping soiled feet in squirming bowels
picking lost paths to seedless farms
with the silent echoes of lost spirits
red eyeballs scrub red sun and hearth
and I must satisfy these hungry gazers
leaf by the wayside waiting for rain
but hot urea steeps the parched field

> as guns of Butare lie silent.
> The guns of Byumba are silent.

beneath the anthills of Kagitumba
below the mountains of Kajumbura
new hills swell to flesh challenge
and the waters dyed, curl up and die
hyena calls hyena over abundant flesh
the vulture soars towards the west
above the nightmare wails in Bugarama
we claw back the mysteries of life
pumping through both doors to dust
our teeth flashing, our lips parted

> while the guns of Byumba lie silent.
> so the guns of Gitarama are silent.

and there is no birdsong left in Muhamba
only the rattle of fresh bones scattering
and crowding to crown my memory of song
I hide beneath the sanguine soil
watching the approaching phantom
she stretches her hands to heaven
she pries the earth with cracked feet
she calls their names above the din
but no heaven or earth has gods to hear
only lost shadows in search of images
in the sudden human mounts of Ruhuma

when the guns of Gitarama lie silent.
The guns of Gikongoro are silent.

yet the rusty machetes are rehoned
yet the rusty machetes are rezoned
across these dusty shelters of Goma
I sing to a mother beneath the ground
I sing to a father beneath the ground
but only echoes rock the caves of Kanembe
searching for pathways to memory
searching for wheat germ among sand
bulldozers sift the dead from stone
to create new borders for the dying
and sites for scavengers of sorrow

as the guns of Gikongoro lie silent.
The guns of Ruhengeri are silent.

brave zoom lenses arrange doomed limbs
as liners for the cloaks of laughter
with abundant myths and silent dream
I am among the bewildered souls, blank
groping for warm unhacked links
with their sudden departed flesh
in the grind of the sinking axe
in the gush of the sanguine flood

as the guns of Ruhengeri lie silent.
The guns of Kibungo are silent.

I sink beneath the ruins of Busasamana
I sink beneath the stares of Nyabyanda
I sink beneath the raised arms in Akayoku
gasping for dry land in swirling Kivu
but the whirlpool of extended thumbs
throw broken nets that web my strokes
as they bow apologies to each other
across the tired spasms of my hiccups

18 Carnival

> and the guns of Kibungo lie silent.
> The guns of Kigali are silent.

so I alone stand with the horizon
singing to our labyrinth of sorrow
but my song re-approaches me
but my song re-approaches me
among whitened bones
winds blow before me
across my paths of retreat
winds blow after me
I squat astride our stripped name
and call your name Oh Rwanda! Oh Rwanda!
land of my bitterness! land of my birth!

breaking termite subways

in power spaces

seeking my security

in distant embraces

looking for my shadow

in foreign faces

but sufferation sits

in these places

but lamentation leaps

in these places

over these powdery bones of my liberation
when Oh! the guns of Rwanda lie so quiet.

Wendy Agnew

HOW TO MAKE LOVE TO AN ANGEL

First you lure
them down from
heaven with
promises of goodness
and weeping.

Then when you feel
their feathers are brushing
against your face in
the dark you sigh
and wonder aloud
about clouds and vapour
and yesterday's icons
about the colour blue
and greenery and ivy
which grows up up to
their domain...
About Venus and whether
they know her and
about the sea shell she
rides on and have they
ever done that and
whether they were there
when Zeus changed himself
to a swan and made love

20 Carnival

to Leda and is it
bad and do their delicate
wings wither from sin and
is sin red and wine-soaked or
is it grey and husky dusky
like ashes and nuclear winter.

And then you feel your hands
on their hands and their little
fingers flutter like moths and
their hair curling up
like blue fire not smoke
and their mouths
not even visible from being so long
in the dark and then you have
to grind your genitals into a fine powder
to fling across the sun so God
coughing and wheezing is
distracted from
his voyeuristic pursuits
and the angel
snickering with mischief
trembles in your breast
inside the prison of your ribs
so the fluttering of its feathers
lifts you to the moon
past the steely rankness
of the righteous   past the tiny
trampled brain of conscience
and into the vast unconscious
of the unimaginable infinity
that lives

beyond the beyond the beyond

   the beyond   the beyond

     the beyond the beyond

         the beyond

from THE LILLIAN LECTURES

OK Lillian Pillian Rillian
listen to this:

Mothers and fathers have
a pact with the devil
When they decide not to become
nuns but to get married
and have sex because *that's*
where we get babies
The devil makes the man
swallow a frog on
their wedding night
that's why your father
burps sometimes and
the woman has to swallow
a spider. Then the
frog and the spider crawl out
and look at them when they're
sleeping and see what they
look like and then the frog
spits on some dust and
the spider weaves the
dust and spit into a baby that
looks sorta like your mom and dad
then the spider drags it back inside
the mommy's tummy.
That's how you got born
pretty neat eh?
Now the baby grows inside
there cause your
mom catches flies and
eats them at night
when nobody can see
her

22 Carnival

OK that's why
mothers are always swatting
flies in the day time — to
build up a supply so
the spider keeps weaving
the baby   and when the
baby comes out there's
this cord on it from
the web and when they
cut the cord the
poor spider dies

When I have a
baby I'm going to keep
eating lots of flies after the
baby's born so my spider can
still live

Geese have long necks

why?

cause they
are God's
spies and
they look up
nuns' dresses
That's why Mother
Goose has all
those stories
cause up nuns'
dresses is where
all the best
stories are.

Norbert Schmidt is a
German. His dad
was a Nazi in WWII
and killed a bunch of people
with pills that turned
into bad air
Norbert says all those
dead people come into
his room at night
and it's so crowded
he can hardly breathe
and he has to sing
them lullabies till
dawn for them to go away
Norbert's mother drinks beer
and sings Santa Lucia
in the back yard and
his father is in prison
somewhere. She feels
bad she chose such a
loser for a husband

so she's making a new
one out of lint from
the dryer. She's naming
him Puffy and she's
making him have no
arms and no mouth.

Matthew Remski

from DYING FOR VERONICA

35.

Veronica, I list your apparitions, miracles, and cures on uncured vellum. I roll it and bind it with a lock of your hair and send it to Rome. The messenger drops dead in the Sistine Chapel after handing it over. The pope kicks the messenger's corpse in bored disgust. The pope yawns and scratches his ass with the crook of his staff. The pope opens my envelope. The hair inside gleams. The Holy See is blinded. He staggers in latinate execration. Technicians cue the disco balls, which pop out of the genitals of frescoes. Choirboys break into a howling triumphal march to divert the cameras.

We used to play Space Invaders for hours. They lined up like the armies of angels in 50s catechism texts. We took turns sliding our lego-esque avatars along the bottom of the tv, sending up slow bolts of love into the bodies of light, right between their feelers, which opened and closed with metronomic sexuality in a programme of flight. We killed thousands at a time, getting better, always better, winning more and more Time in Space, winning the illusion of better and faster weapons to combat the illusion of more intelligent, more malicious Foreigners.

65.

The long bow of my body, left by a mute hunter who's retreated to caves to nurse a lonely hunger.

I lean against the stone-cold drywall and look out through the kitchen window. The cup of my shoulder turns to metal and siphons the ice. The fires of winter smoulder in trash cans. All the lawyers are hard at work. Today is a bad day for tv.

Yesterday, however, I saw this nature show. It was about songbirds. I thought it was totally appropriate that the ornithologists just can't figure out why songbirds migrate.

They return to Northern Ontario in April, having flown 9,000 kilometres from various oases south of the equator. They stop in central Mexico, Texas and Kansas. Some veer east, lighting upon our fair city's High Park in fatigue and near starvation. Fifty million birds pass through each of the main arboreal pitstops per day, over a two-week period. Two hundred and fifty species are represented in the migration. And now, in 1994, only half the numbers are flying as when the ornithologists started counting and tagging them in '63. No one knows why the numbers are diminishing.

The average male songbird sings over ten thousand times a day.

The show featured clips of a volunteer bird counter and his wife who have been assigned a 40-kilometre stretch of northbound highway to monitor each spring on behalf of the Canadian Songbird Preservation Society. They climb out of the van at intervals of 800 metres, she with a clipboard and stopwatch, he with binoculars. He is given three minutes to name all of the birds within earshot. "Begin," she says, clicking the stopwatch. He calls out. TWO RED-BREASTED WOODTHRUSH

FOUR, NO FIVE MOURNING DOVES OVERHEAD
ONE CATBIRD
THREE LYRE-BIRD
ONE PARADISE HAUNTER

THREE GREENBACK FINCHES I THINK NO IT'S FIVE I'M SURE IT'S FIVE and "Stop," she says, jotting the last entry. He never uses the binoculars, but cups his hands to his ears. Interviewed later, he says *Well each bird has its own song, and they're all quite different. Some even use different dialects for different reasons. Anyone can learn these languages if they really desire.*

26 Carnival

72.

Veronica, I have been writing these true things for seventy-two days from the same room. I ask for no remuneration. Writing is not a profession any more than bleeding is. Those who do it for money are much bigger liars than I. That's why they get hired by Reuters and AP. — The sky is bloated with sky-descriptions, signifying a general cultural unwillingness to look at the immediate materiality of, say, our hands. — My hands... hmmm. My hands are my hands.

I learned to type in a class taught by a nun. No secular textbooks were allowed. The exercises were taken from prayers.

Sister Evangelica barked out the letters and directions for arranging the prayer on the page:

CAP Hail SPACECAP Mary COMMASPACE full RETURN
of SPACE grace COMMASPACE the SPACECAP Lord RETURN
is SPACE with SPACE thee PERIODSPACERETURN
CAP Blessed SPACE art SPACE thou SPACE among RETURN
women COMMASPACE and SPACE blessed SPACE is RETURN
the SPACE fruit SPACE of SPACE thy SPACE womb RETURN
CAP Jesus PERIODSPACESPACECAP Holy RETURN
CAP Mary COMMASPACECAP Mother SPACE of RETURN
CAP God COMMASPACE pray SPACE for SPACE us RETURN
sinners COMMASPACE now SPACE and SPACE at RETURN
the SPACE hour SPACE of SPACE our RETURN
death PERIODRETURNTWICE

By the end of that year the opening exercise of each typing class was the every-letter-in-the-alphabet drill: **Saint Zoe sang that Jesus leaps down from the crucifix whenever the martyrs beckon the quick to love.**

The final exam consisted of typing out the entire mass in Latin, with the correct capitalization and spacing, again while looking only at the crucifix. Sister saying, Remember, if one letter is out of place, it is not a mass.

As the time wound out and my mistakes became more frequent I wondered whether a whole room full of boys with hard-ons and girls with sweating backs typing out **HOC EST CORPUM MEUM** could make something happen in another part of the world, or even here, the newsprint with fuzzy lettering transubstantiating into silk, leathered skin, the perfect veil. (— I saw a deaf woman this morning talking to herself in sign language. She was so graceful. She was whispering to me: *This is what typing is, dear.* Her hearing aids shone like snails.)

Patricia Seaman

from SUPER NEVADA

I had expected him to avoid the usual places for a while, but no, I was wrong. I imagined I could walk around like that. No one would notice. He, of course, would never see me. One of the things that I had done in the weeks that followed, during what I called *my holiday*, was have my hair cut. I did it by accident, without my own consent. It was against my own wishes. I was overwhelmed by grief. At the time I didn't understand it. I didn't know what I was doing. I didn't like it but it was too late. It was impossible to reverse time.

I had slept in and was late for work. I got off the streetcar and walked the last block to the café. I was rushing. The leaden ceiling of the early winter sky was as oppressive as those words that had never been spoken.

It was then that it happened. I was surprised when I saw him. Nothing could have prepared me for it. A tremor ran through my body.

He stopped. He stood in front of me. He prevented me from walking on.

Hello, he said.

He had the tact not to mention my hair. He avoided mentioning it. He was afraid of what it meant. That I'd gone mental. That I hated him. He couldn't help looking at me, though.

How are you? he said.

I always forgot everything. It caused me all kinds of problems. I forgot what he had said to me. I couldn't remember if it had been at the restaurant or when we had gone for the walk along the lake. I didn't know when he had decided or if he had given me a clear indication. I had overlooked some crucial remark.

I let things happen. I had no opinion. I watched it all with my eyes wide open in surprise. I went along with it like a little tourist.

I'm well, thanks. And you?

When we first met I had talked to him a lot at the beginning but it bothered him so I soon gave it up. By the end, nothing. It never occurred to me to reproach him. It wasn't his catastrophe. It was mine. There weren't any words to describe it. I knew it in the finest detail without words. It appeared to me as an image. It was so brightly illuminated that it was agonizing for me to look at. There was nothing I could have said to him then. Not one thing. And anyway, it was all in the past.

I continued to stand there, smiling. I was in shock.

He too smiled. He radiated good health. It was obvious that he'd never been more cheerful.

We both acted perfectly friendly toward each other. He a bit more so than me. There was an edge to my voice that I couldn't hide. The less I said the better.

He pointed out that I'd put on some weight. It looks good on you, he said.

I felt like I could have stood there on the street all day talking to him without saying anything important and watching people walk past us. However, he was in a hurry.

If I could have said anything to him I might have said, thank you. That's all. Or, thanks for the drink.

He wouldn't have had any idea what I was talking about. He would have thought I was being melodramatic. When we had been together, even at the very beginning, he used to look vaguely hurt and uncomprehendingly at the things I said. It made me want to laugh my head off.

I just got back from Montreal, he said. It was great. I had a great time.

He smiled. He had something to tell me. He was bursting with some good news. He was debating whether to tell me what it was or not.

I smiled, too. What is it? I said.

He pretended to misunderstand me. Then joy won out. Slyly, he said, I'm in love.

I must have stared at him for a very long time. I became aware of certain signs of discomfort in him. The shifting of his eyes as if he were searching for something under dim lights. The movement of his body at first inclined slightly toward me as if in supplication and then rocking back on the heels, holding the head as far away as possible, wary.

After another moment of silence, in which the noise of the street passed through, it occurred to me that he was waiting for a response. Under the circumstances I had no idea what I was required to give. I didn't want to get involved. I gave that which had the least to do with me.

I'm happy for you, I said. I have to go. I'm late for work, I explained. Goodbye and good luck.

Sometimes I wanted to go to Emergency. But only to sit quietly on the plastic chairs in the waiting room. Only to wait, without clamour, for the morning. Fear prevented me. I was afraid of being caught and mistaken for a chronic case. I was afraid of the metallic clean taste of the doctor's hot fingers forcing *chemical kisses* between my lips.

All I wanted was to be beautiful. In the way the hippies said, a beautiful person.

Stuart Ross

AROUND THE BUILDING

From across the road,
I peer at the building.
It is grey, it
rises nine floors.
I work in it. I work
five floors up.
My watch tells me it is 7 a.m.
At 8:30 I will be at my desk,
and I will take the top sheet
from a pile of paper
and I will scrape specks
from it with a special little knife.
It is my special little knife
and not one defect will go by
unscraped. I am the best in the world
at this. But now,
it is 7:02 and I cross the road
and approach the glass doors.
I light a cigarette, like I do
every morning at 7:02,
then I light another, jam
another in my mouth, and
another. I walk to the left,
to the edge of the building,
and I turn the corner. I walk
to the back of the building,
and I turn the corner. I walk

across the back of the building,
around the dumpster, then
turn the corner. I walk
to the front of the building
and turn the corner. Soon I am
at the entrance again. I look at
my watch. It is 7:09. I walk around
the building again. It is 7:17.
A bird smashes into a third-floor
window and falls to my feet.
I place it in my pocket and
circle the building. It's a different
bird from yesterday. My pocket
is getting full.

I smoke and I walk, and I trace
my hand around the brick. This
building contains me, contains
my thoughts. This building contains
my desk and my phone, my special
little knife, my cubicle. I smoke
and I walk, walk faster, and the traffic
grows. My co-workers begin to arrive,
slipping silently through the door.
I walk around the building. It is
8:26. In four minutes I will be at my desk,
clutching my knife. In four minutes
I will know what to do.

Velvet Curtains

They are making hamburgers from vegetables, from beans!
Lord, I never thought I'd live to see the day.

In the cinema, I sit in the front row,
and the flickering screen is so big,
Robert Mitchum's shadowed face so vast,
I gotta tilt my head way back
till in the ceiling I see chiselled LOVE and HATE.
A rope unravels, dangles
before my eyes. I take hold
and am lifted, slowly towards the ceiling.
I pass by Shelley Winters' glistening brow
and feel popcorn rain on me like kisses.
And when I reach the rafters and the lights,
look down upon the crowns of 100 heads,
a woman with hair of seaweed takes my hand,
says, "Hey, it's good to have you back among the dead."
And she shows me how the velvet
curtains work, the mysterious
velvet curtain mechanism,
and we glide across the ceiling
like we're at Arthur Murray's.
"It's cloudy here," I murmur because it is.

As she brushes the cloud from my hair,
I admit that once I drove a bus
and wore a moustache. I wandered through the forests
singing hymns. I slept in a barn
and counted sheep to sleep.
"Abide the children," she said,
"the gentle shivering omelettes." And I —
I who once across the river leapteth —
I knelt, undid my laces, and exhaled.

Eileen O'Toole

FLORIST

I was out with my boyfriend Lester and we were at the florist, picking out wreaths for his mother's funeral. We had fifty bucks and wanted something real nice. Lester wanted a horseshoe to wish Mom off and I kept thinking that he's burying a person, not a horse, and seeing as we can't afford a gravestone or plaque, I thought we ought to get one of them bull's-eye circle wreaths and put a plastic bag over it in the winter or something. Anyway, we looked around and things looked pretty steep so we looked in the freezer room for something to do. We walked around looking at the bunches of different flowers, some were tropical and kinda horny looking. Then Lester calls to me and I go over and there is a Macedonian hyacinth. You know, it's not at all like the flower we call by that name, but it's shaped like a lily, and it's deep purple or, like, splendid crimson. Lester sighed and said that I was really like that flower when I danced — frozen.

SAM'S

I was out with my boyfriend Lester and we went into Sam the Record Man's store. I do and I don't like going into Sam's. Sometimes it's real crowded, like when Metallica's LPs come out and it's kinda fun to be surrounded with, like, the same kinda people who have good taste and like Metallica. We'd all be singing and pushing and looking at the liner notes. Then sometimes I'd go in and it would be real nice and quiet. And just the right band over the speakers and the aisles would be empty and you could just look at the store and the records. Of course, you wouldn't have to read them or anything, but you can just look.

Record stores got a kinda strange, funny magic about them. It's kinda like you could fall in love in a record store, or you could commit suicide in there, or genocide, or nothing could happen and you could just say, "Shit, this is just a bunch of filing cabinets sitting around." Then you say to yourself, Hey, no, wait, this is, like, history. This is the place where you come where, like, you can find the band who, like, was playing and, like, doing something when you were born and you can trace, like, the whole of mankind through a record store. So you think to yourself, Wow, like, Sam's is almost sacred. It's history in the making. My history.

Like, I just made this stuff up myself, OK? Like, I never even went out with somebody from there. I mean, it wouldn't have been bad, you know, there are some cute guys and you could probably get some deals. But I mean that I think about having a philosophy for this place, because it records the world's major influences. I never go into the classical music section. It scares the bejesus out of me. I like looking into it. The rest of the store has the same feel, like a basement, but walking into the classical stuff, it feels so strange to have the ceiling way up there.

Jaymz Bee

CLINT EAST WOODY ALLEN ALDA

I wanna be a jazz legend, a master of impressions
I wanna inspire a symbol and give aerobicize lessons
Buddy Rich Little Richard Simmons

I wanna be a little bit girly, then act like a stud about town
Wear a glove, have a chimp, and make folkie type sounds
Boy George Michael Jackson Browne

I'm havin' a celebrity identity crisis
Feel like Milton Berle Ives or Buck Henry Fonda
Star struck outta luck I know I'll never be
Lenny Bruce Lee Marvin Gaye, William Conrad Baines
or Clint East Woody Allen Alda

I wanna have big hair and big teeth, I want Cher to have my baby
I wanna wear sunglasses, while watching lotsa TV's
John David Sonny Bono Vox

I wanna be a Canadian native, a French babe at a beach blanket bingo
I wanna shout punk philosophy, using conspiracy lingo
Buffy Sainte Marie Antoinette FuniCello Biafra

I'm havin' a celebrity identity crisis
Feel like Elton John Wayne or Buddy Guy Smiley
Star struck outta luck I know I'll never be
Willie Nelson MandElla FitzGerald Ford, Billie Jack Lord
or Freddie Prinze Charles Nelson Reilly

I'm havin' a celebrity identity crisis
Feel like Brian Keith Moon, Salvador Dali Lama
Star struck outta luck I know I'll never be
Pat Say Jack Palance, Jim Carrey Grant
or Clint East Woody Allen Alda

André Alexis

PIERROT

1. Queen car, westbound to Lansdowne, 2 a.m.

For a moment, there, I was almost happy...

Not that I'm able to identify the state with confidence. It's been so long since I was happy, I don't miss it anymore.

I have moments, of course, when I know I'm missing something, moments of reckless optimism during which I tell myself: it's all a matter of attitude, smile, let yourself go, the people in Cambodia have it worse, that's for sure. Then, with effort, I curl my lips. And sometimes, I even feel the old fluttering, like wings in my rib cage. But even those forced emotions are rare, these days.

Still, for a moment there, on the Queen car, westbound to Lansdowne, I was almost happy, without trying.

2. The moon, from behind a cloud, moments later.

A woman, looking lost, crosses her legs, and looks out the window.

I scratch my neck. My eyebrows need straightening, so I surreptitiously straighten them. I'm reacting to the woman, of course, and I resent it; resent myself, I mean. At the first whiff of womanhood, I go through the ritual motions of grooming. It's too late now, of course. If I'd wanted a woman, I should have showered properly, straightened my eyebrows, scratched my neck, hours ago. It's no use going through the motions now.

The scratching and straightening aren't going to make me desirable at this point. Just the opposite.

3. The moon obscured, minutes later.

— Can I see that transfer, please.
— Transfer?
— Let me see your transfer, please... This says six o'clock. It's no good.
— Why no good?
— It's expired.
— Why expired?
— If you want to get on, you'll have to pay your fare.
— But I have transfer.
— It's expired.
— Why expired?

It is winter. The recent snow has melted and the streets are slick. The tall, thin black man pays his fare. The woman for whom I've straightened my eyebrows uncrosses her legs and pulls her coat tighter. For a few moments, as the streetcar rattles past Gladstone, I lose track of my whereabouts.

I can't afford to lose track. My stop is only two or three away.

And then it occurs to me, I don't have to get up. There's no one waiting for me. I could go to the end of the line and come back, enjoy more-of-the-same for a few hours, a leisurely return to my basement. Put off the decision to wash the dishes, at this late hour.

Really, I should have washed them earlier. If I'd wanted clean dishes, I should have washed them hours ago, before going out. But no...

I went out, hopeful that this gathering would not be as desolate as every other gathering I've attended...

Why should I wash the dishes?

4. An abandoned building, boarded up, seconds later.

I've had some alcohol, but I could still masturbate, though if I've had too much to drink, I won't enjoy myself. I might manage an erection, but even if I do, I may not be able to do anything with it. Perhaps it depends on the alcohol. I drank Scotch, but I don't know which drink is the greatest inhibitant. Am I less prone to erection after Scotch? Beer? Are all drinks equal, where tumescence is concerned?

And then there are the women of my "triple-x" videos. I've seen them so often, it's as if we were married. I feel I am doing a duty, masturbating to *Nice Buns* or *Truth and Dare*.

Frankly, it's no longer pleasurable.

Perhaps the alcohol has spared me the tedium of my baser instincts.

5. O'Hara Street, as the night air pushes into me.

As I step down onto the street, I feel like a mouse.

The light from the twenty-four-hour donut shop catches my attention. The street I have to walk is dark and empty, though there is one man, moving unsteadily, on the other side of the street. He looks taller and stronger than I am.

If he crosses over, in front of me, I'll cross to the side of the street he's abandoned. And if he crosses again? Can I cross back without insulting him?

If I cross the street and he realizes I'm avoiding him, I could provoke resentment. Resentful, he would have legitimate grounds for an assault.

But, if he wanted to assault me in the first place, my crossing the street would only make matters plain to both of us.

There's so much to consider where human relations are concerned.

Happily, he falls to the pavement. It looks painful.

— Ohh…, he says, and lays there.

Well, that's it then. Another transaction avoided.

There's no one else in sight. Clear sailing from here on home.

And again, despite myself, and perhaps because of the alcohol, I feel a brief lightness.

It amazes me that I have my good days.

Elise Levine

TRUE ROMANCE

Another woman shaves her legs, bites her lip. He must be sleeping, this room she's walked out of and left for all she knows for good. All night lone birds smoke from the maple at the end of the drive, something she has thought a long time: a fast car, long white fingers on the wheel, Niagara Falls to Eastern Avenue. At the end of the Lakeshore the Cinesphere floats kisses she could scale, kisses fat as a baby who won't be born though slugs thicken like sex on the sidewalk and stars, stars' fat fists shake

up.

Untitled, artist's collection

Every morning, the old towel, furry and moss-stained. She'd hold it open and wait. Her mother in the water holds one arm up, one arm down, swims out like she's beating eggs. Then her mother swims back, hardly moving, eyes closed and breasts barely visible above water. Hold the towel open, mother's long wet hair falls across skin the colour of parchment, the raised surface a braille of goosebumps.

One fall morning her mother was gone, drifted so distant only to surface, later, in the town bars: bare trees, brown earth, and everything silent except the bumping of the canoe all afternoon against the dock.

She grew up on that island. Her father's landscapes utter a pigment, blemish, for each of root, tree, sky. Late into November his paintings tumescent with colour against the back door where he first piles them, then they slowly upholster the walls of the cabin. She spent her winters dizzy with the slow wandering urge of oil and turpentine.

Her father's skin around her like a canvas. Pulls it tight across her shoulders on cold nights when the lake crisps to curls of black through the trees. Loosens it, too, lets it drape across her bare shoulders when she takes that one behind the beer store parking lot. How she spent her sweet sixteen.

Ducks bark in early evening. And later, a billion stars at night in a sky so big it hurts the eyes; she learns to close them. All grown up now. In self-portraits she paints herself crowded into the room. So much colour! Patterns everywhere.

Though the dead still tap her brush — and it's nothing, no colour, white canvas leaking aimless blank shapes — as they did once last year when she stayed alone in the old cabin for a week.

Winter framing her like cold white sheets in an old bed.

This Is It

I never thought you were the one for me. You climbed out jilly-jam fast, four legs waving. New. You pulled me up with you, uterus trailing black-green, ice blue, pink: the electrics of me. Coding splashed the walls. My call stung the mattress like salt. I smelled bad down there. Lick it, and sometimes you did. There's no such thing as one perfect skin, ocean, the thin plankton bloom I'll always remember you for, kelp forests surging through the room and the funny greenlings and wolf-things, eels. My bound breasts. There's no such thing, I've got it all wrong, there's no miracle I can't make right again. This is it. I drag for miles in the net of your sweat your glitter, poised above me on your elbows and the small packet of sperm you'll check later for how much or how good. Darling believe, you'll say, this

is as good as it gets

John Barlow

THE HAPPY IDEA

Human beings are through and through
Crippled with remorse, corrupt, evil,
Possessive, slandering, ill, warped,
Cut   into   shreds,   despairing,   hopeless,
Heartless, vicious, unthinking, uncaring,
Unweaned & self-centred, & blind, blind...
Human beings are bleak sheep & sheep stink
And dying, dying; of spiritual starvation:
And they are, and they are, and they are...

Forever in a moral dilemma over it,
Forever denying it, concealing it, sinking into it,
Letting it crush their experience and joy of life into
Misery, and mine, mine... mine, mine.
Letting it crush us in months of depression,
Decades of disease, hours of failure,
Moments of hell, I love... you... anyway...

Letting it kill and go on killing,
Besieging it to kill, defending its right to kill,
While forever moralizing... whimsically about it, in-
Decisively pandering to it, rationalizing it,
Reconstituting it, in delusive and formal
Life-denuded breath-denuded, empty, stricken, language.

...While the weak and the vulnerable are punished,
And the sweet and the innocent are entered by death,
O snakes o greyskins o scum,
Why Don't You Shoot Yourselves in the stomach
In the heart or in the head, instead of...
Shooting yourselves in the sexual organs
And then, o summer, denying it hurts,
Instead of shooting your wives
That know the truth about you,
And claiming temporary insanity,
Instead of shooting your brains near numb and nearer
Worthless, and pretending it doesn't matter
O you sick dullards you businessmen
You beefing asshole boors, o gods

Let me tell you of a place I went to
In a dream. It was a good dream...
But as with many, as with dreams in life,
It started poorly. I was outside,
Nervous frightened and alone, and black tadpoles,
Black tadpoles, which became eels,
Black and lascivious and entwining,
Were all about me, swimming in my eyes,
As I stood within, with my heart gulping
For air, an upright, glass coffin.
Such that I, when the glass coffin vanished
But the eels did not, fell into a ditch.

Somewhat ashamed, entirely defenceless
I remember falling and asking a woman whom
Intuitively I did not distrust, for help.
And she helped me, helped me get out,
With as little prolongment, as little embarrassment
As possibly I could have hoped. It was wonderful
It was wonderful o joy o goddess

44 Carnival

And this then was the crazy winter I had met
A whole new generation of friends of the family
Who had invited me with familiar voices to swim and fish
In their complicated backyards with the waterworks
And to run — gallop — between narrow fences over mud quickly.
The year was 1998 I presume, as the flooding was not yet
So accustomed, whole garden parties consisted of little more
Than the marvel at so much water.
There was a freshness of amusement in the air
Such as I long for, even now.
That night in the cool dark of their glassy den
They had let me to myself to enjoy freely
Their supersonic tv and to
...gather
recollections
of an earthly
community...

> A celebrity drug addict was being interviewed
> On his own terms in the bleachers of the ballpark,
> The game on, it Friday night, relaxed television broadcast
> Diverted by curiosity to the patrons in the stands
> Telling how and when and why it had started,
> Finally growing angry, child-like, demanding his drug
> And there was no moral underline, only the friendly and benign
> Tolerance one so easily forgets can occur
> In the annals of (   ) man...

O kind race, O, kind, kind, possibility
We had Open State, the Planet of America
A coldless winter, everyone happy and honest and guilty

A group of businessmen on the train
Invited me into their cabin
To read pamphlets on tax and insurance fraud
Put out by the government
Which encouraged short-lived wealth as a means
To psychological prosperity
And to join with them in happy fraternity
Concocting correlated madhatch stories
With which to blame the fire at the well
On the one man who was there and smiling along
With shameless depravity of confidence in his juror's
Forgiveness, not for the money but for the glee of it!
There was much free laughter and champagne
It was wonderful. But as I woke Christ said *No! Interpret it*
Differently, but it was too late, I was loving it too much,
I was actually loving humanity; beautiful, young,
Playful humanity. Everything overwhelmed with water the
Landfill clogged lakes dancing like jellybeans on my table
And everything else giddy during the earthquake

MONDAY, JULY 18, 1994
ATTENDANCE: 800

Bill Kennedy

from APOSTROPHE

you are a deftly turned phrase, an etymological landscape, a home by the sea • you are a compilation of more than sixty samples overlaid on top of a digitally synthesized 70s funk groove • you are the message on a cassette tape long after it has been recorded over • you are, as such, the eraser head's self-validating ideal of order • you are a festering war wound incurred in a skirmish between the U.S. and Canada over rights to a pig farm strategically located on what is now referred to as the world's longest undefended border, making you a better meteorologist than any one of the "big three" networks, or the CBC for that matter, can muster • you are used & abused • you are a distress property bought by Tom Vu & sold for an outrageous profit • you are ossifying sweat on Robert Plant's performance towel, now in the possession of a man who is thinking about auctioning it off because he has decided he would rather listen to "new country" • you are an onion ring with an identity crisis on the Korona Restaurant's "Transylvanian Meat Platter" • you are an easy-riding h that just knew you would be stopped by police, cuffed, hauled in & strip searched while you were making your way through the mountains in Georgia • you are everything your mother had hoped for, & more • you are track-lighting gone bad, a one-time energy saver now driving a gas-guzzling '71 Impala • you are considering touching that dial • you are a pretence to universality • you are the top quark • you are one of a family of Dirt Devil™ carpet cleaners • you are wondering at this moment whether you are merely a cleverly disguised rip-off • you are a foreign agent who accidentally ruptured an emergency cyanide tooth cap just before your rendez vous with a thin man in a lumber jacket standing by a garbage can on the patio of a McDonald's in Paris, who was to receive an attaché case containing vital information photoreduced on microfilm

50 Carnival

which, of course, you have no prior knowledge of • you are a mispronounced word with eyes stuck in an awkward position, just like your parents warned you they would, trying to get a date with one of the "cool chicks" in your high school & having a difficult time of it • you are fibre ingested by a septuagenarian to promote regularity • you are a face in the crowd • you are secretly responsible for both the mysterious circles appearing overnight in British grain fields & getting the soft-flowing caramel into the Caramilk™ bars • you are not using the Force, Luke • you are fucked up in your own special way • you are toiling, neither do you spin • you are an immediately perceptible phenomenon elevated to the level of theological unity • you are accurate to a depth of 30 m • you are pecs on your pecs • you are thrown out for lack of evidence • you are a nested loop • you are getting sleepy • you are an ode to the west wind • you are made in your own image • you are wanted & loved …as if • you are a case of halitosis, gingivitis, dandruff & split ends all rolled up into one • you are a granny knot undone by an older & wiser scout leader • you are a piece of performance art that deep down inside wants to be a bust of Beethoven sitting on a Steinway grand piano • you are a primal scream trying to differentiate yourself from an existential scream • you are a hockey stick broken over the spine of a 19th century hunchback you figured had no business playing street hockey in the first place • you are a healthy Hi-Pro™ glow • you are having paranoid delusions that a figure much like Henri Matisse's "Blue Nude" is following you around trying to get you to join the Jehovah's Witnesses • you are the distance between the hyperbolic curve at the y-axis • you are what you eat • you are a reified universal transcendental signifier • you are kind of pissed off that you were never given the choice of whether to be a sequitur or not • you are, and if you aren't, who is? • you are not enough to get over the threshold • you are getting even sleepier • you are a fine piece of work, you are • you are a stupid English k(o)n-ig(g)ht • you are a 60-cycle hum • you are a refutation of the Special Theory of Relativity • you are a parade of endless details • you are the lusts of your father • you are wondering at the audacity of some people who like to tell you just who they think you are • you are synaptic information lost in the aphasic shuffle • you are a means of production • you are the line cut out of the final edit by some guy using a PowerBook in a cheesy local Laundromat, or if you aren't you wish you were • you are being completely irrational • you are the wrong answer on the multiple choice section of the LSAT • you are feeling quite overwhelmed • you are exactly what they've been looking for, and that should frighten you • you are the significant answer in an ink-blot test • you are well on your way • you are the space between the heavens and the corner of some foreign field • you are rendered completely useless • you are a B- grade on a C paper • you are so beautiful, to me • you are unconsciously acting upon your cultural biases • you are a game of tic-tac-toe that, after dealing with an inferiority complex, beat up a game of "globalthermonuclearwar" and kicked the shit out of Pentagon computers • you are on your way to the store to get a litre of milk, when this cow with the head and antlers of a moose sporting black eyepatch over his left eye comes up to you and says "you are on your way to the store to get a litre of milk, when this cow with the head and antlers of a moose sporting black eyepatch over his left eye comes up to you and says "you are… • you are the weak argument in an elaborate doctoral thesis • you are the miracle cure for halitosis, gingivitis, dandruff & split ends all rolled up into one, at least that's what your 19th century procurer, "Dr. Morgan," says as he travels from town to town trying to sell you • you are not but let's say you are • you are your favourite letter of the alphabet except *h* cuz that has already been taken • you are an asshole • you are a soliloquy on a barren heath in a play which inspired Shakespeare's "King Lear" but has been lost for many centuries, last documented in the Earl of Derby's private collection, 1723 • you are billed as the "nicotine patch to the world" • you are everything you want in a drugstore • you are only as good as the next guy • you are the eggman, you are the eggman, you are the walrus (kookookechoo) • you are shovelling shit in a Roman stable • you are dead now, so shut up! • you are in the process of being palimpsested • you are an incestuous mess • you are available only through this limited TV offer • you are the party of the first part • you are a no-good, lazy son-of-a-bitch • you are often replaced by an apostrophe • you are a big waste of time • you are a poor player who struts and frets his hour upon the stage and is heard no more • you are surely mistaken • you are a detachable penis • you are therefore you think • you are the side effects of performance enhancing drugs • you are a bad case of blue-balls • you are boldly going where no man has gone before, but only as the disposable crew member who happens to be dumb enough to talk to a lump of painted grey styrofoam & therefore, in my humble opinion, deserves to get it anyway • you are translated into 20 different languages • you are not smart, just hard working • you are a painting bought solely for the frame • you are the one who really likes it, *really* • you are not a machine, you are a human being • you are corn, but

52 Carnival

we call it maize • you are dumb enough to spend your time typing out endless statements that begin with "you are" just to make a point and try to get some laughs, neither of which, in retrospect, you believe you will succeed in • you are the owner of the secret decoder ring, and as such have a right to be president of the club • you are the interest accrued overnight by some clever electronic banking maneuver • you are, and if you aren't you should be • you are misspelled in a grade six spelling bee by a kid who will eventually serve 8 years in jail for manslaughter • you are better than bad, you're good • you are a quote within a quote desperately trying to escape • you are a most noble swain • you are in absentia • you are engaging in self-nullifying behaviour • you are a vague sense of alienation masked by a friendly, conversational atmosphere • you are the kind of apathy that can only be generated by the "spoken-" vs. "written-" word debate • you are a self-consuming artifact • you are an unimportant stanza in an unimportant Bob Southey epic • you are the neurochemical dopamine bridging the gap between the tail of one synapse and the head of another during a bout of particularly raunchy sex with a not-quite-loved one • you are an instance of pre-emptory teleology • you are living in a post-theory, post-language writing, post-sound-poetry, post-literate age, so let's stop writing crap that pretends that you aren't • you are a reference to the font size of this poem • you are going to sell out the first chance you get • you are yawning — stop it! • you are a persnickety line removed at the friendly request of an editor who thinks its potential offensiveness is enhanced by the mere fact of its referential obscurity • you are all out to get me, damn you! • you are mixing memory with desire • you are sitting with a soggy ass at some reading in High Park really wishing you were somewhere else • you are a portable Greek reader that is going to party like it's 1999 • you are going on with your doggy life • you are the interplay between the quotidian & the extraordinary • you are a ravenous, meat eating carnivore who lusts after the feeling of animal blood tracing the crevasses of your chin, or if you aren't, you know one • you are a Captain's log, supplemental • you are a metonymic slide • you are a pipefitter with a penchant for Descartian ontology • you are everyday people • you are believing this crap they're feeding you • you are convinced you looked better before the makeover • you are an uninterrupted series of dots that hasn't come to terms with being a line yet • you are an ill-used neural cluster removed to get at a deep-seated brain tumour • you are fading away when you would rather be burning out • you are a linguistic trap set to catch some good eatin' possum • you are eleven benevolent elephants • you are drool currently stringing its way to the centrefold of a porn mag • you are a registered trademark of the Coca-Cola corporation • you are the supreme arbiter and lawgiver of music • you are woman, hear you roar • you are never going to amount to a hill of beans in the world • you are bad advice foisted on some love-sick puppy • you are an axiom proved false • you are the cruelest month • you are an error in grammar identified by the latest in word processing technology • you are flown to your destination on Delta Airlines • you are the book in the spirit machine • you are a dadaist who needs to love & be loved • you were preconceived by both Boethius and William the Conqueror yet still have no clue as to what surrealism is really on about • you are in more closets than you wish to admit • you are someone with the debilitating habit of cutting against the grain • you are going, going, gone • you are a likely consumer of rubber nipples • you are a long-lost jazz score that no one would have played anyway • you are a last will & testament • you are an unceremonious exit

Nancy Bullis

LINSEED OIL

It's been seventeen moves in fifteen years
few consistencies
except maybe a lot of time buying things and throwing them out
something I had to go through to find out what's important

A knife, a fork and my old schooldesk from days of ink wells

One of my first acquisitions and I still haven't refinished it
simple, solid oak
it would be easy to do
a little linseed oil and a few Saturday afternoons

It's amazing what time can do when you polish the same spot
that's what he was trying to tell me
eight years ago
that long to understand

Delayed reaction
there is no refund for time spent on foolhardy purposes
no other way it could be
it was necessary to process
something I didn't put any value in
process
always looking for the newest colour
the latest song

I thought it uninteresting to watch something grow

I had my first fire in the fireplace last night
stoking the embers
I ran out of wood
I could only poke for so long before all I had left were dinosaurs
extinction hasn't stopped scientists from searching for what went wrong

I've been blaming myself for my own conservation

The pictures aren't on the walls yet
each time the choice changes except for a few
the dog, the boy with the wine, and Churchill

Picked Winnie up for the price of the frame
the essence of the man
understanding failure
didn't capture me until after our days dating in a cartoon land

We created story board characters thinking
reality took care of itself

I thought some guy in the sky was going to save the world

Books are easy to unpack
not much thought to know where they go
except if it's alphabetical, chronological or by genre

My dream was to live in a science fiction theme park
being an alien from another planet
always looking for
the time of teleports or
the place John Lennon wrote about

"Imagination isn't always a good thing," he'd say, asking.
"when's dinner?"

"Only mortals eat," I'd say,
a fundamental difference in our lifestyles

56 Carnival

I know how to make simple meals now
what it's like counting vitamins

I didn't know how satisfying limitations could be

I like to eat goat
something I didn't have the patience for as a child
always lifting the lid

"How long will it take?"
"Is it done yet?"
"Can I go now?"

As an adult
I leave when I please
not always understanding that
time is the greatest reasoner
not to say
that I left too soon
or I shouldn't have at all
or it took too long to recover

No one can say when is right

Acceptance begins with yielding to what can't be forgotten
about myself

Just like that old schooldesk

On Saturday, I am going shopping
for a little linseed oil and a chamois

Death Waits

BREAKING SKIN

"It is possible that the atmosphere or the earth's crust requires a certain quantity of human blood to satisfy its chemical or other interests." — *Karl Heinzen (1849)*

this poem resembles a personal anecdote I find slightly embarrassing, so embarrassing that when I have tried to write it in the past the results were either hackneyed or so opaque as to defeat the entire purpose of the exercise... childhood is like that: beyond the reach of reason, far more important than writing

without the hard edges of full blown theory reality withers — and tell me that story again and again and then never again: how the funeral of the theatre director was packed (but then closing nights are always packed, I thought aloud, careful that no one heard me) and for hours on end I stared at the stained glass windows — for though they gave me no reason to be sad — others were crying

I remember writing that we are in 'for a millennium of unparalleled bloodshed' • that blood is the carrier, the victim and the sacrifice • that from one vein to another one travels on one's knees • that the immune system is not a metaphor because without it bodies crumple away like so many tears in an abandoned handkerchief • that I bleed from every orifice and not a single drop is sacred • why did I write those things?

prick my finger, re-read hegel, wash the dishes — to make everything more complex while at the same time reducing it to its essential horror — to calm the nausea of believing, bleed away to nothingness, recall whatever passes for 'worth remembering,' see a show, the show, any show, be stood up by the person you could never really love while standing in front of a restaurant, lit by sunlight, forever

58 Carnival

the embarrassed anecdote of the introduction involves my childhood best friend, an ice-skate and my face: you can read it while examining my features, a scar across the left diagonal, dried blood on the blade, friends die almost every year now... blood glistens on the surface of water from a time when water wasn't water yet, sharks circle, needles inhale, scars are stitched, sealed and forgotten

a sprained wrist among the plague, a black eye during the holocaust — but closing nights are always packed — tears of a madhouse becoming photographs I wish I had taken and again: becoming, bleeding away, the world, forgive

GOLDFISH LOVES WOLF

Instead of killing myself
I bought a goldfish
and watched it swim around in its little bowl

It's just like me, I thought
swimming around in its little bowl
and when the fish spoke
it spoke of the wolf
and when the wolf spoke...
but no, the wolf never spoke

Death Waits 59

So, instead of killing myself
I bought a tiny goldfish…
every time I changed the channel
it made a run for it
startled by the flipping noise of stations exchanging
it would tell me things about myself
how I was isolated and brilliant and sad
and should feed it tiny flakes of algae
three times a day, religiously

The wolf would hide behind the television set
(occasionally venturing inside
for the warmth and comfort of communication
they both so craved)
always watching
my every mood and move

Wolf wouldn't whimper, wouldn't sulk
wouldn't growl
only think of eating me
the way I might taste
juicy with blood
as it watched me tap three servings of survival
into the goldfish bowl
whistling to myself
while it quietly grumbled:
that's it, stop dawdling
hurry up and kill yourself
you stupid poet
I'm hungry

Lise Downe

Déjà Déjà Vu

in this wonderland of doubled vision
everything can only stammer
tossed from hand   to
                hand   to
                hindsight an extraordinary talent
where escape isn't a dream
and where virtually every tradition is based
on absence
a continuing first take
evoking images   it's not clear
but in any case wondering
if it might be the fragile edge
along these margins that run
      raw and restricted
and which then slowly dissolve into the rough idea
or subvert a symmetry
        (however profound)
for "reality" tropics even the sceptic
with proof enough
                a few sun-warmed berries
                and a discreet elegance
                besides

WEATHER I

within the solid and simple
within the deep and growing calamity of propulsion
there is cause to justify contrast
between fact and fiction

we have never known
how fluctuation takes refuge in miracle
for now a final day
easing toward self-portrait

if there is a moon
it is infinitely coloured
it savours a developed passion with humour
inscribing astonishment
all alluring and moody as any arching projection
will ever be

now switch and witness the wicker's whiteness
after a long silence inspired to hold
its green interwoven then cascading
and everywhere awakening
each morning with each hour
shifting calendar upon an offshore breeze
vanilla   haltingly

unfamiliar appearance that seems somehow
appropriate
prolific and profile steady
reaching out to touch   to touch

but will an upset bucket and no money
fall back upon symphony or indigenous rhythm?
the first canto...

62 Carnival

but who's counting?

there is at least one thing
the sweet and precise
subtlety
meaning a gradual dawn that may eventually confirm
this premonition of a summer's hurricane

it, like the haunting phrase
could let slip a wealth of coining
"value" and "invention" divided into three parts
both unique and startling to the naked
I

I of the storm that
is

Rafael Barreto-Rivera

from SHREDDED WHAT: A WHITMAN SERIAL

(1)

Among the anguish-centred, the brotherly, the writerly,
nature with all its breaks, you have one decent
option: impersonate yourself. And then
what follows:
assume, and every hazard befits the
crescent change
   and what   an arrogance
   for every atom
to you belongs, good as to,
what and, observing summer's fine
     "brutally spiritual"
the same parents there and, the same from here born
parents of here born
     retiring
 bad, good,
impaperfections, protocopies
unprecedented, preparing
arts & inventions,
religions & literatures,
politics, "new"
again primal, exciting,
expanding

64 Carnival

You, too, along
with impedimental limp and "speed
                              impeachment,"

"organcized"*
news-addict,
                    infomaniac
gathering processing transferring and delivering

          sanitized exchanges/propagender

   And you're over forty now, keeping up
the fight
long enough to make
        a fucking difference

(2)

houses   rooms   andgasms (a definite
improvement)
shelves
books   speech   reach   radio silence
my need, a fever   the promotion of the
"blue-haired & blondeyed"
and a shelved poet and a talking one,
      both getting at
                    the average meaning of poems.

You know what the happiest thing about you is?
That you are who you are, and it is written
all over your face

---

* I am indebted for the two terms in quotes to Mr. Ed Allenby, with whom I once
worked.

(5)

you, the you you'd like to be
    not words   not music   very random-access-like
carnal reproduction   DNA paragraphs
"sensing device that
    can measure speed, distance, etc."
input-output of
                your self-monitoringness
        peering into a screen
        the screed —
  these binary
        reductions/refractions/reflections:

mental floss.

            Not sure of anything,
enjoying ritual portions,
            you dash, forsooth,
Into the vomitoria

66 Carnival

(6)

Wordgasms & thoughtgasms
        vagina pectoris
            angina dentata

(not to dwell on
            the subject of
                vagina envy*)

    Give us, oh Lord
instead of capitalism
            carnivalism,
or something like it:
        a language based upon
    essential proteins
                proleptic fictionary
        edging toward some kind of
redemptive password
(*in hoc signo* vindicated)
                breathe-write

fullscale dis-erasure/integration

    Go back to first elastic zygote

tool around

        and change

    the look of everything

---

*Years ago, I said to a poet friend: "For years I have suffered from vagina envy."
He referred to this exchange, subsequently, in a poem of his.

M. Nourbese Philip

DISCOURSE ON THE LOGIC OF LANGUAGE

WHEN IT WAS BORN, THE MOTHER HELD HER NEWBORN CHILD CLOSE: SHE BEGAN THEN TO LICK IT ALL OVER. THE CHILD WHIMPERED A LITTLE, BUT AS THE MOTHER'S TONGUE MOVED FASTER AND STRONGER OVER ITS BODY, IT GREW SILENT — THE MOTHER TURNING IT THIS WAY AND THAT UNDER HER TONGUE, UNTIL SHE HAD TONGUED IT CLEAN OF THE CREAMY WHITE SUBSTANCE COVERING ITS BODY.

English
is my mother tongue.
A mother tongue is not
not a foreign lan lan lang
language
l/anguish
  anguish
—a foreign anguish.

English is
my father tongue.
A father tongue is
a foreign language,
therefore English is
a foreign language
not a mother tongue.

What is my mother
tongue
my mammy tongue
my mummy tongue
my momsy tongue
my modder tongue
my ma tongue?

I have no mother
tongue
no mother to tongue
no tongue to mother
to mother
tongue
me

I must therefore be tongue
dumb
dumb-tongued
dub-tongued
damn dumb
tongue

EDICT I

*Every owner of slaves
shall, wherever possible,
ensure that his slaves
belong to as many eth-
nolinguistic groups as
possible. If they cannot
speak to each other, they
cannot then foment
rebellion and revolution.*

68 Carnival

Those parts of the brain chiefly responsible for speech are named after two learned nineteenth century doctors, the eponymous Doctors Wernicke and Broca respectively.

Dr. Broca believed the size of the brain determined intelligence; he devoted much of his time to 'proving' that white males of the Caucasian race had larger brains than, and were therefore superior to, women, Blacks and other peoples of colour.

Understanding and recognition of the spoken word takes place in Wernicke's area — the left temporal lobe, situated next to the auditory cortex; from there relevant information passes to Broca's area — situated in the left frontal cortex — which then forms the response and passes it on to the motor cortex. The motor cortex controls the muscles of speech.

THE MOTHER THEN PUT HER FINGERS INTO HER CHILD'S MOUTH — GENTLY FORCING IT OPEN
SHE TOUCHES HER TONGUE TO THE CHILD'S TONGUE, AND HOLDING THE TINY MOUTH OPEN,
SHE BLOWS INTO IT — HARD. SHE WAS BLOWING WORDS — HER WORDS, HER MOTHER'S WORDS,
THOSE OF HER MOTHER'S MOTHER, AND ALL THEIR MOTHERS BEFORE — INTO HER DAUGHTER'S
MOUTH.

but I have
a dumb tongue
tongue dumb
father tongue
and english is
my mother tongue
is
my father tongue
is a foreign lan lan lang
language
l/anguish
　anguish
a foreign anguish
is english —
another tongue
my mother
　　　mammy
　　　mummy
　　　moder
　　　mater
　　　macer
　　　moder
tongue
mothertongue

tongue mother
tongue me
mothertongue me
mother me
touch me
with the tongue of your
lan lan lang
language
l/anguish
　anguish
english
is a foreign anguish

EDICT II

Every slave caught speaking his native language shall be severely punished. Where necessary, removal of the tongue is recommended. The offending organ, when removed, should be hung on high in a central place, so that all may see and tremble.

70 Carnival

A tapering, blunt-tipped, muscular, soft and fleshy organ describes
(a) the penis.
(b) the tongue.
(c) neither of the above.
(d) both of the above.

In man the tongue is
(a) the principal organ of taste.
(b) the principal organ of articulate speech.
(c) the principal organ of oppression and exploitation.
(d) all of the above.

The tongue
(a) is an interwoven bundle of striated muscle running in three planes.
(b) is fixed to the jawbone.
(c) has an outer covering of mucous membrane covered with papillae.
(d) contains ten thousand taste buds, none of which is sensitive to the taste of foreign words.

Air is forced out of the lungs up the throat to the larynx where it causes the vocal cords to vibrate and create sound. The metamorphosis from sound to intelligible word requires
(a) the lip, tongue and jaw all working together.
(b) a mother tongue.
(c) the overseer's whip.
(d) all of the above or none.

Nino Ricci

from I AM SALMAN RUSHDIE

The last thing Tony Darcangelo expected to see, riding east on the College streetcar toward work in the stifling August heat of a morning rush, was the flash of a knife. He might not have seen it at all, if conscience hadn't kept his eye shifting at each stop from the book he held open in his lap to the throngs of newly boarding passengers in case some invalid or old person or woman with child should board to whom he'd feel obliged to surrender his seat (though when just such a candidate got on at Bathurst, the frailest of old women with a silver-headed cane in one hand and a tiny lap-dog, of all things, in the other, it was the teenager in purple mohawk in the seat in front of him who beat him to the punch); but suddenly there it was, emerging from the crush of bodies surrounding him like an image you'd read about in a story or see in a dream, several inches, though afterwards Tony couldn't say how many, of cold silver metal, and all of them coming toward him with what looked like brute, unswerving intention. Almost in the same instant that Tony saw the knife, someone — or so Tony assumed, through the inevitable gestalt of extrapolating from a voice a human source — leaned in close to his ear and whispered like a secret the words 'There is no God but God.'

And then the deed was done, a quick entry of silver and exit of silver-red. Tony's first reaction was straight out of the movies, after all the only place where he might have drawn a role model for this sort of thing: without a sound he stared down at his chest and brought a hand up from his book to touch the blood that had begun to seep out of him there. His second reaction, too late, was to look up to see if he might catch sight of his assailant. But before him was only the usual wall of insensate torsos, and then directly in front of him the blue hair of the woman with lap-dog. He had sufficient presence of mind then to turn his head toward the centre exit doors — the streetcar had just pulled up to a stop, and descending the steps was the black-haired back of a head that looked, perhaps, a bit more agitated than that of the usual downtown commuter; but through the thicket of bodies that blocked Tony's view of the windows on the exit side of the car he got no further glimpse of the head as the streetcar pulled away from its stop and continued on its route.

I ought to scream or something, Tony thought, but that seemed a little melodramatic now already so long — it felt like hours, weeks, millennia — after the fact; and it was a testament to Tony's discretion, and to that of his fellow riders, that the streetcar had travelled another full stop before anyone noticed what had happened. By then, Tony, the first frugal bloom of red on his shirt quickly burgeoning to mutant proportions, had begun to grow faint. The book he had been reading still sat open on his lap, a few tiny circles of blood bedecking the pages it was open to like spatters from a fountain pen; though as Tony himself began to droop the book slipped an inch, then an inch more. Then at last the book was airborne, though with what seemed to Tony an almost slow-motion languor, closing discreetly on its blood-speckled pages as it rounded his knees and then flipping, once and once again, a lovely arabesque of motion, to land finally with an impossibly distant thud on the flat of its back at Tony's feet. It was only now, with the cover of the book directly before his eyes like that — and it was not that Tony had chosen to look at it, but that the book, as Tony slumped and his consciousness ebbed, had fallen precisely in the spot where the pull of gravity had gradually inclined his gaze — that Tony made a connection, just before the world went black, between the book, the knife, and the six words whispered mysteriously to him; for the book staring up at him was none other than Salman Rushdie's infamous *The Satanic Verses*...

Tony had actually met Salman Rushdie once, and this post-fatwa no less. It had been about a year and a half before at a benefit for a writers' human rights group at which Tony — who liked to think of himself as a writer, though this was not a fact that he made public any more, as he lacked any evidence to buttress it — had volunteered to work backstage. No hint had been given beforehand of Rushdie's appearance, of course; though when Tony had shown up at the stage door to take up his duties, two men in grey suits had questioned him extensively and had been on the verge of turning him away, despite the fact that his name appeared where it should on their list, until the benefit's organizer, the publisher whom Tony worked for, had materialized to vouch for him. Odd, Tony had thought, confused but also not a little miffed by the whole episode; and it was only clear to him afterwards that what had probably so concerned the men had been his swarthy, nay even semitic, appearance.

The benefit was a sort of cabaret where various writers performed acts they lacked any real skill at. At half time everyone involved was gathered backstage and the twenty or so grey men who had been hovering around them the whole evening talking into their sleeves were posted at all the exits (they were there because the premier was coming, it had been put about, no one bothering to speculate how ludicrous this suggestion was); and then suddenly he was there among them, looking dishevelled and jet-lagged and human and yet all the more impressive for that. Tony hadn't dreamed of getting near him; but then in a lull that he'd noticed often befell writers of stature at events such as this, he found himself suddenly alone with him. For a moment he stood in thrilled, terrified silence; and then an inspiration came. Like nearly everyone else present, Tony was wearing a button, part of a campaign started a year or so before, that read 'I am Salman Rushdie'; and it suddenly occurred to him to make some joke about how in medieval battles several knights would dress up as the king to confuse the opposing forces.

But what he said was, "So what do you think of the buttons?"

Inane, inane, he thought, as soon as the words had left his lips; and Rushdie stared at him with a look of such intense bewilderment that his worst suspicions were confirmed.

"I'm sorry?" Rushdie had said, and at that instant Adrienne Clarkson had suddenly reared up behind him and whisked him away.

What Tony thought about now, however, as he lay in his hospital bed, was not Salman Rushdie, or that night; what he thought about was the knife. Real knife or imagined one; angel of mercy or angel of death. What it had felt like as it had wedged its way between his ribs. There had been pain then, that was true enough, pain such as he'd never known, pain that had beggared him, that was the only explanation for his otherwise unaccountable silence. But there'd been something else, too, a thrill at least as big as his pain, the thought that had burst upon him like a revelation that after this there was no going back, that everything he'd known in his life till then was on the brink of some catastrophic, magical, wondrous, unthinkable change…

Karen Mac Cormack

SOME MILES ASUNDER

Based on letters written by Lady Mary Wortley Montagu on a journey to Constantinople, 1716-1718.

my project in one word is not for so much I

Some blew as three at daybreak even	*Rotterdam*
in a few days of abruptly	
with his hours altars she less days	*Nimeguen*
a dozen to in touching	
ever with seven from titles consequence	
all canals	
one bridge	
broad-brimmed mind given to Lorraine	
the I is to hat	
a motion from to quarrel.	

Cologne

One almost lemon so the most as squeezed	
when a time down those diversified	*Nuremberg*
in far number one	
pleasant, impertinent, monstrous as fortified art	
gilt machines of the German curtseys	
contrary with cover of	
enough comedy made numberless, upright	
visit can defend the taste	*Ratisbon*
swiftness too a fort.	*Vienna*

Whole entertained divide but several
carried imitation passed this merely   *Prague*
ripe use after with the vases, but other growth of so
might statues own excessive moonshine   *Leipzig*
than town effect and near an absence
is in all with an inch Chinese
no candlelight and come the same cannot   *Hanover*
indecent between the hints
five times foundation wear diverted.

Hunting but they obliging cannot by snow
these regained until or abandoned anywhere the passports   *Blankenburg*
whatever, half nothing pleasure
with conversation hold the fruit as something till translated
Rousseau places seventeenth   *Vienna*
side apartments call parting quantity
eight are an affection to the south rebellion
almost fifty to act winter the air only
deposing towers, repaired, adjusted wolves   *Peterwaradin*
satin to reason with some scraps of history.

                                                              Belgrade
Though not through glasses intermixed roof as next falling
confused this colder since your poetical running
by informations word
considerable mysteries side guess every unheard of   *Adrianople*
troublesome ten o'clock
in plain Titian they believed
without paces shade steams in discovery.

76 Carnival

Horses, turtles, storks walk generally very two
first adjoining to other insteps
large trees, ladies, mosques   *Constantinople*
distinct, the garden arches, vines, wall round scene
public extremely
without fear the cause that painted glass
more chairs
in the lower parts of a fond chiosk and honeysuckles
though an opera unacquainted with
laborious innocence of many inconveniences
will last down galleries
of ten twining sort of to this last
the globe.

Concluded kneeling and soon the very house
that almost entrance of on steps
any little motive dressed
and handkerchief
with guitars saying the difference   *Belgrade Village*
a pavilion increased or four seemed raised with her so much
more than ambassador to other number
this custom spice sweet water up.

Wholly some extravagance thinking when   *Pera of Constantinople*
covered the camp
tents drawn in slashed advance
after taken up, turn of most polite we call vanish
I see their diversion near
all present followed
trickling play over finest dare or amuse with street
after him a windmill
one trade faces this gallantry
of honour looked upon not spoken of
japan in my own language.

Last to first
surrounded order: the body
a raised white, outside *I*
but they
all for court with cloisters pavement vastly high
the gardens are to see
Persian toy-shops of lesser size
summer as the way cypress
neck and turbans
notwithstanding heats, who swelled with this
the distant
divorced their stiffness an Englishwoman and a place
fields occasion letters
Black Sea for all that equal balm
(extraordinary formality in that affair)
a bed of Asia larger on top of it the voluminous dictionary
up fifty steps.

These in a harem
of rooms at velvet knowing
a pearl, cinnamon, gold, postscript pepper
but a Turkish clove, a match, wire (in a box) ever   *Tunis*
the love-letter
jonquil, gold thread inking and Friday least the air   *Genoa*
paper, hair, fingers performing giddiness, the language
pear, grape, soap, coal, a rose, a straw, cloth.   *Turin*
                                                                          Lyons

78 Carnival

From where to now every Cleopatra (not so miserable)   *Paris*
all in Versailles staring
not from geography
with forced tranquillity particular on faces
good night drawn over blind never lifted
and seven being unstable
count that form
to elephants, salt ponds
of this (till) absurd beautiful rate
three, and count them!
crystalline lattices, tapestry of mouth nothing in it
religions to tulips, alternate agonies   *Dover*
with our scanty allowance of daylight
I would
but suppose you
if he
after me.

Al Purdy

AT THE QUINTE HOTEL

I am drinking
I am drinking beer with yellow flowers
in underground sunlight
and you can see that I am a sensitive man
And I notice that the bartender is a sensitive man too
so I tell him about his beer
I tell him the beer he draws
is half fart and half horse piss
and all wonderful yellow flowers
But the bartender is not quite
so sensitive as I supposed he was
the way he looks at me now
and does not appreciate my exquisite analogy
Over in one corner two guys
are quietly making love
in the brief prelude to infinity
Opposite them a peculiar fight
enables the drinkers to lay aside
their comic books and watch with interest
as I watch with interest
A wiry little man slugs another guy
then tracks him bleeding into the toilet
and slugs him to the floor again
with ugly red flowers on the tile
three minutes later he roosters over
to the table where his drunk friend sits
with another friend and slugs both
of em ass-over-electric-kettle
so I have to walk around
on my way for a piss

80 Carnival

Now I am a sensitive man
so I say to him mildly as hell
"You shouldn'ta knocked over that good beer
 with them beautiful flowers in it"
So he says to me "Come on"
so I Come On
like a rabbit with weak kidneys I guess
like a yellow streak charging
on flower power I suppose
& knock the shit outa him & sit on him
(he is just a little guy)
and say reprovingly
"Violence will get you nowhere this time chum
Now you take me
I am a sensitive man
and would you believe I write poems?"
But I could see the doubt in his upside down face
in fact in all the faces
"What kinda poems?"
"Flower poems"
"So tell us a poem"
I got off the little guy but reluctantly
for he was comfortable
and told them this poem
They crowded around me with tears
in their eyes and wrung my hands feelingly
for my pockets for
it was a heart-warming moment for Literature
and moved by the demonstrable effect
of great Art and the brotherhood of people I remarked
"— the poem oughta be worth some beer"
It was a mistake of terminology
for silence came
and it was brought home to me in the tavern
that poems will not really buy beer or flowers
or a goddam thing
and I was sad
for I am a sensitive man

MY GRANDFATHER'S COUNTRY
UPPER HASTINGS COUNTY

Highway 62
in red October
where the Canadian Shield hikes north
with southern birds gone now
thru towns named for an English novel
a battle in Scotland and Raleigh's dream of gold
— Ivanhoe   Bannockburn   and El Dorado
with "Prepare to Meet Thy God" on granite billboards
Light thru the car window
drapes the seat with silken yard goods
and over rock hills in my grandfather's country
where poplar   birch   and elm trees
are yellow as blazing lemons
the maple and oak are red as red
as the open mouth of a dinosaur
            that died for love
of eating

Of course other things are also marvellous
sunsets happen if the atmospheric conditions are right
and the same goes for a blue sky
— there are deserts like great yellow beds of flowers
where a man can walk and walk into identical distance
like an arrow lost in its own target
and a woman scream and a grain of sand will fall
on the other side of the yellow bowl a thousand miles away
and all day long like a wedge of obstinate silver
the moon is tempered and forged in yellow fire
it hangs beside a yellow sun and will not go down:

82 Carnival

And there are seas in the north so blue
the small bones of the brain take on
that same blue glow like unto a fallen sky
they speak of the illimitable
those immense spaces of nothing and nowhere
the mind can scarcely comprehend
so far beyond human touch we must rely
on impersonal science
to tell us of shimmering violet meadows
and comets visiting earth and returning at such measured intervals
the ancient rememberers were long since dust
and we cry our name to the stars and the stars
do not remember

But the hill-colours are not like that
with no such violence of endings
the woods are alive
and gentle as well as cruel
unlike sand and sea
and if I must commit myself to love
for any one thing
it will be here in the red glow
where failed farms sink back into earth
the clearings join and fences no longer divide
and pour themselves upward
into the tips of falling leaves
with mindless faith that presumes a future
and earth that has discarded so much so long
over the absentminded centuries
has remembered the protein formula
from the invincible mould
the chemicals that after selection select themselves
the muscles that kill and the nerves that twitch and rage
the mind-light assigned no definite meaning
but self-regarding and product of the brain
an inside room where the files are kept
and a little lamp of intelligence burns sometimes
with flickering irritation that it exists at all
that occasionally conceives what it cannot conceive
itself and the function of itself:

the purpose we dreamed in another age and time
an end just beyond the limits of vision
some god in ourselves buried deep in the dying flesh
that clutches at life and will not let go

Day ends quickly as if someone had closed their eyes
or a blind photographer was thinking of something else
it's suddenly night
the red glow fades and there is no one here
but myself and I am here only briefly
and yet I am not alone
Leaves fall in my grandfather's country
and mine too for that matter
— later the day will return horizontal and gloomy
among the trees and leaves falling
in the rain-coloured light
exposing for ornithologists here and there
in the future
some empty waiting birds' nests

Susan Musgrave

OUT OF TIME

Who plans it, whoever looks
up at the stars the first time
and thinks they've seen it all.
Same thing, night after night. Nothing
astonishes them. No, the first time
you look at the stars you think
you, too, could live forever. You're parked
at Cattle Point in his Chevy Bel Air
smoking your first cigarette, drinking
Cinzano from the bottle while he points out
the Big Dipper, the Milky Way
before slipping a condom over the tip
of his brother's service revolver and making you
take it down your throat. The stars
blink out one by one as he starts to push
harder on the back of your head, spinning
the barrel, thinking because you let him
kiss you once it meant you wished to go
even further. "I'll make you a star,"
he says, pulling back on the hammer;
you're running out of time, out of breath.
He lights his last cigarette, and you
relive forever in that moment, waiting
for the click.

ARCTIC POPPIES

After a week of rough seas the ship docked
at Hopedale. The weather was no good but still
I struggled ashore and climbed to the desecrated
churchyard, determined to take away something
of a memory, to photograph the white Arctic
poppies. Each time I framed a shot, my hands
steady at last, a hunchback on crutches teetered
into sight, as if innocently waiting for the fog
to lift, the rain to let up, the light
to throw open its dingy overcoat and expose
itself to my nakedness. My eye, my whole body
had been saving itself for this, but every time
he humped into view, I thought of you, the best
man I'd ever left, lips tasting of whatever you'd had
to eat: spicy eggplant baba ghanoug, jumbo
shrimp in garlic and Chablis, your mother's
savoury meat pie with a dash of cinnamon
and cloves, or , the morning after, eggs
over easy and bitter coffee. When the sun broke

through I'd have those wild flowers posed,
I'd be poised to shoot and then the stooped
shadow would fall as if to say beauty
without imperfection was something to be
ashamed of, as if he could be my flaw.
Crouched beside an abandoned grave
I tried to focus on those white
poppies in light that went on failing,
seeing your perfect body in his
crippled gaze. I could have taken him

back to my cabin aboard the ship, laid
his crutches down, bathed him, bent over
his grateful body and licked the smell
of smoked trout and caribou hide from his
thighs. Perhaps this is what he hoped for,
and then to be called beautiful afterwards.

86 Carnival

I took his photograph. He'd wanted that, too
and suddenly I felt blessed, I felt
I'd been taken the way I liked it best. Sex

in the head on sacred ground that has been
roughed up a little, a graveyard full
of ghostly poppies choking out the dead.

Water Music

In Spanish prisons the "water cure"
was used to determine innocence,
the prisoner bound, mouth held open
by a sharp-edged prong. A strip of linen
conducted water into the mouth,
like a stream like the swollen stream
you have chosen to picnic beside, wiping
clean the faces of your young children
with cool linen smelling of warm fruit
and later, in the hottest part of the day,
watching them strip and plunge, breathless,
into the water, each one determined to stay
under the longest causing the victim to struggle
and choke. You look up from your book, almost
loving the way your children can hurt you,
their sharp-edged joy.

"Time to get out of the water!"
you cry, as they disappear a final time,
their innocent mouths opening then closing.
You try to explain cruelty to yourself,
but there is no cure: you watch them break
from the surface choking no no we don't
want to go not now. Yet you know you have
already outlived your children as they dive
and scream in your bloodstream slipping away.

HOLY GROUND

for Arlene Lampert

We left the literary party Al Purdy
had invited us to in some sad luck Toronto
hotel, picking our way over the drunks who had fallen
asleep on the stairwell, through the ladies
of negotiable virtue outside. You made me
hold your hand, you in your mini leather coat,
me an innocent from the Queen Charlotte Islands
in my flowing gown and the Irish widows' shawl
I always wore back then as if I had looked
into the future and seen what was in store:
where would our love go, what were we headed for?

We made a pair! Old laughing girls we dubbed
ourselves Wardey Birdsong and Blossom Endrott
for the evening, imagining for the moment
what it felt like to be wholly desirable.

I wanted to look them in the eyes, these hungry
men under the Nudes! Nudes! Nudes! and All-You-Can-Eat
Pizza signs: I'd thought of men as our allies.
Don't look at them, you hissed, gripping
my hand harder. Instead of cutting through
the unlit lot to our car you said we would skirt
the whole block. Neither of us knew this was Hog Town's
Holy Ground; we trudged the oldest known gauntlet
of sneers and solicitations, non-literary
invitations we pretended we didn't understand.
"If you won't fuck us," they cried, "fuck you!"
Oh, Wardey, I whispered, *what should we do?*

You always knew what to do. And that's how
I still think of you, strutting way up ahead,
defiant, no shame on you. You always knew
where we were headed, too,
didn't you?

Mac McArthur

WE SAT IN OPEN FIELDS

i

Pneumonia is a final drug
but I watched a slower death.
That afternoon I rubbed
a back and younger neck.
Mostly bone, he nodded thanks.
They called me late at night.

This morning, that evening, his dawns
        and my nights are plugs into time.
Their pulls are circles spinning clockwise,
hypnotic to a drain.
Remembrance is a dying word.

I disagree with time.
Birthing is over too soon,
living once, not forgotten.
The heart I grew was legs into life.
The cord cut was formal, not real passage.
We did share every vein.

A dead son leaves no future,
only pasts in drawers.
I wear moments:
the traffic, this fog.
His silence kicks inside.

90 Carnival

The litmus of lichens
turns to pink or blue,
acids and the bases.
He was both
and moments holding neutral ice
just before its surface drips.

Chills of resonance last
and last and last.
His voice was wire, thread,
adventure: strident May marches,
then soft as coming sleep.

ii

Sheers trapped his bed
as he came face to death.
Pale horses and names children call
flew past on lyric heels.
I waited for one lid to lift
    to remember clouds we watched
        confront the moon.

One night we sat in open fields
to share the other's sky.
Clouds ran from lunar winds
behind the moon (so it seemed).
They never ran that way.

Dark as cirrus ice,
they ran a far eight miles
above the earth
(invisible in that bright circle).
I said the light we saw was China's sun.

Full ignoble moon reflects a source
(never creates her own).
The clouds we chose as ours
came out whole the eastern side.

iii

My father used to wonder
if his brother's grave had trees.
My son offered colours without occasion.

Over olive porcelain, waterlilies floated
(ordered to open before I rose).
Pussywillows scratched Japanese bamboo,
white paws of windless kites
stretched a binding string.
Odd fragrances bore no message.
With blue iris, he held Spring.
Gladioli wore new crimson,
purple, black and saffron powder.

Irregular blooms of children leave home,
fall into mirrors,
rise out of tablewax,
are gently gone,
discarded gently.

A painless brief exit has never been built.

iv

His body loosened, lost its hold,
tumbled sinking, rested final.
    Mid-ocean air free-fall
    snapped slow by nylon,
    floating to land on water,
    sinking reflections,
    leaden fathoms,
    Atlantis deep.

92 Carnival

The body behind the sheers
lay full aware of steps.
Into unique air between us,
I leaned past thinking for a hand.
His was not wrinkled
(as we laughed I would become
if only age did kill).

I touched his lifeless skin.
It was not what we had planned.
So many holes per inch of gauze,
enough to see both image
and the fact his body was his.

v

The soul is space,
a sphere that grows.
The pole I fixed
was no more than a womb.
    There, midnights are dawns.
    There, dark is still the same as light.
    There, half a bodyturn
        is ten thousand miles of change.
    There, direction unlocks time.

But I have no idea what order is to be.
Rows of like objects fall in line
    one after the one before.
No quiet nights bequeath days never started.
No years point to single losses but at all.
In me there is no fool, only split time.
I know the cord from there to here.

The wind that bows is friendly once,
but no wind bows twice in one direction.

Nancy Dembowski

MIRROR WRITING

I have begun living in fear of nothing,
certain my death has been revealed to me,
pouncing up, paranoid,
not of ghosts, but of the sleepless,
                    the literal,
and dreams of my right breast,
your finding a lump,
            the size of a small apple
you believe me now (about the numbers being transposed
and my daughter's mirror writing)
no symbol of free-floating anxiety
having joined my brother's wife,
what is left of my sister's friend,
"but she's had seven children"
and Kelly, in her wisdom,
"we must cherish that which gives us life"
both the globe and the apple of eden,
the sickness that feeds a whole planet,
healed with radiation,
                    a figure
            [of the end] of everything...

BORDERS

The walls are nearly naked;
just the edges of clean paint, where absent pictures
frame my children and half a dozen out-grown playthings.
We pretend to watch his composition of magnetic letters;

The b means nothing

without the e.

Even now, we barely contain ourselves;
pushed to the corners, you slide your hand beneath my blouse.
My breasts, will miss you. My fingers,
caught between the glue and paper,
extract the letter:
month old mail;
in black, as though in mourning,
(I forget what shoes or dress it was exactly).
Out of shock, or habit, I entered it on disk;
as though inscribing, in memory, would erase, somehow, its meaning.
I cut out words, bits of syntax;
effaced the fable of the princess
who gained microscopic vision from
a tower with twelve windows.
What she wanted most was freedom.
And thus, decreed, that any suitor,
who could not escape her vision,
would lose his head in trying.

97 heads stood in rows before her castle

— the border of her freedom —

And who will you construct of me from memory?
In whose imagination will you bury our existence
in patterns of your language?
Letters repelling and attracting;
little fingers move the o beneath the r and form a gibbet.

Should I say my country needs me?
They are starving out the children,
as I wait halfway the distance, of indignance,
and the horror, of the bones beneath my babies.

Should I write that I am screaming?
Or absent myself from presence?
The children won't recall, that we once lived here;
so I must paint for them your vision,
from the road maps, of our teardrops,
in the absence of your letters,
I was always good at acting.

GHOSTS

I find her in the kitchen, waving a paper fan;
his letter, a love story,
psychologizing her personality.
We toss the coins, and here he stands:
the one who tore her dress and his friend,
who stalked at night through tombs,
and dug, with sticks, her childhood,
buried in toys and poppies under the willow tree,
weeping, he coaxed her into the office
    and made her research graves late into the night.
He thought her brave, face down,
his breath against her back, liquid scalds her scalp, she laughs,
    she can not help herself.
And now, across Formica,
she takes my confession, as she took the Sunday bus,
a girl in blue velvet, me in my best:
daring the hung over chalk, the one who tore her dress and his friend.
Closing the morning's coffin with cinnamon and prayer
I find her in this place,
she rests, amid the roses, dead weeks, and petals in her hair.
Have you seen my father, mommy dear?
I toss her high, the way she likes it.
Laughing, laughing, we search the wicked earth in morbid detail.
It's been years, it's been years.
And she's the sign he is returning, coming to find me, in this ghetto,
    this black hole:
wired windows, wired women, women burned with cigarettes,
    blood in a fruit juice glass;
collected, thus industrialized, collaged somehow with absurdities of:
    childbirth, girlhood, womanhood,
        on billboards containing a breast, a thigh…
Car pulls up for a prostitute.
    I take the ride.
        At home, in her bed,
            God is a Bullet on full blast.
                I play the recording twice.

He is annoyed... afraid I am abducted... face down in an alley, or worse...
    reminding him what she meant to him.
I'm hurt, he's cold, he's hurt, I'm cold;
drugged and sleeping he lifts me up like a romance novel and there,
    along the creases of his skin,
        is no part of him I would not touch with a part of me.
He has distorted my industrialization. He has made me.
We crash her grave and she is here, my child, deserted in a borrowed van.
Out-of-rhythm, she drops the stalks in ash, and here the hexagram falls short.
Write the sins you don't remember, he once told me,
and turned the key, and left the motor run;
    ashes spilling over empty letters, barbaric sticks twirling on fire,
        another strange psychology of unending stories...

Steve McCaffery

Novel 39

The world is a room.

There is a single lump in it.

He sees no reason to postpone
the pleasure of the meal she's stepped beyond.

In the sky above moves history's affinity to comas
and there we rest this brute equality
of pronouns.

Martin says it takes
a 90 watt bulb.

Ann tells him to fuck off.

from TEACHABLE TEXTS

A sad passion like performance comes over him.
On a lake of petroleum the words
"command Canada unknown."
So to begin with
how do we escape the clarity of death against
some other dark existence?

Said I to Nietzsche.

The ontology of the neuter looks promising.
It is everything
            and it is everywhere

the universe become a sheet of style
with History folding it into
a bric-a-brac of coups d'état catastrophes.

This is not what Arthur meant
in his lengthy gamatria last summer
thinking,   funny
how it's sort of me
and my precocious femininity
gone wrong
or slightly   misplaced at least
and   surely
related to those things that go bump
in the light.

My personal example of onomatopoeia
is Pinocchio. A pasta that laughs
through its dental geopolitics
of being.

100 *Carnival*

Mince myth with your meaning like this
and you'll find the rubber stamp which fits
your life via gender politics
not Saint Alban's opinions on the mildness
of soaps.

Abstractly conceptual
as in the phrase
punctuality of incompletion?

Sodden on sacrilege and tainted blood
in the back garden of
my either-or
and only three hours twenty six seconds per God.

It's like getting it free for a year.

          It would seem better to shoot poems than to write democracies
and despite being very happy we are extremely pleased
with our space-time continuum
collapsing into Pan-Pacific versions of the dominant
shampoo.

It's sort of like you and cholesterol
upon a midnight dreary, remembering all those things we'd read
in Pope about sylphs with syphilis and hair conditioners
those gossamer toupees on troubadours
and feeling if death should come to vegetarians
via those fast food confusions
then it will all end in a carcenomic
operetta at a fund-raising lunch
the moon rising
a Silken Laumann without teeth
into a bio-hazard danger level 4.
Quoth the raven. Not again.

K AS IN SLEEP

Should find it hard
to relocate between these losses,
veils,
which isn't history.
The primary bigamist and pointing
to canonical attributes
where a body comes undone
conflictual in the mirror's dispossessed
aggressions.

Can't understand
as immobility
the sign
which is
or the hair amongst others
which authorizes
definition.

To turn aphasic.
To frequent language
only when it troubles us.

One is never sure here
of the voice of passion
the televised desire to stay
the child in duty
as a recollection ordered, since
hatred agonized is different
to a scene possessed
then rearranged.

Sonja Mills

I AM SO FAT

I am so fat. I'm fatter than fat. I'm huge. I'm a great fleshy porcine blob of humanity. I'm a house. I'm eight hundred pounds if I'm an ounce. My measurements are 100-100-100. I no longer have a double chin: it's become a second neck. My thighs have thighs.

When I sit flat on a lawn chair, the vast expanse of my ass is immeasur able. Two-four-six feet of bouncing, jiggling, flapping, slapping lard butt; and whereas clever fatsos the world over have invented hundreds of ways to sit in a lawn chair without resting one's legs on the seat, thereby avoiding that embarrassing thigh spread, just try sitting with out the use of your buttocks. It can't be done!

I've always wanted to be big, but believe me, I meant it in an entirely different context.

Oh, the humanity. That mere indulgence in that which I enjoy so much is the very cause of my misery.

Woe is me. That my excessive poundage, and my acute awareness of it, are the very things which cause my further cravings for fatty, deep-fried meat dishes.

Oh, what a cruel joke. That three pizzas are available for the price of one.

I go to restaurants on half-price night so I can eat twice as much.

Oh, and the buffets. Breakfast buffets, pizza buffets, Indian buffets. And Chinese buffets. All-you-can-eat Chinese food. Oh sure, it seems like a benevolent challenge at first. Till you've been there for an hour and a half and you're gripped in the sadistic clutches of "just one more plate," "they're bringing out fresh shrimp," "are those deep-fried bananas?" And just how many honey-garlic spareribs do you have to eat before you can safely say you've devoured an entire pig?

And my girlfriend's no help. Every time I cry to her about how hopelessly obese I am, she says, "I know. It's disgusting. I can't believe how fat you are. You're ten times fatter than you were when I met you. You're grossing me out, you mountain of congealed grease." Her nickname for me is Leviathan. I used to think it was sweet, but now I know it's just a sinister jab at my hulking girth.

Oh, how can she be so cruel when I'm so fat and so premenstrual? Why just yesterday she was an angel. We walked together, laughing and holding hands. Two young lovers on a clear spring day, skipping easily through fields of love, while cool breezes danced their way through the light-weight fabric of my loose-fitting tunic.

But today, those same baggy clothes have become a testament to my expanding frame. I am constricted by the synthetic silk shackles of my enslaving apparel. Oh, gabardine manacles. Cotton-poly blend sausage casings compressing fat and fat by-products into a vaguely humanoid-shaped patty.

Yes, today I am fat. Today the world is a cruel place. Today my girlfriend does not love me. For how could anyone love anything so huge?

> Look into my eyes,
> hear my cries.
> I despise the size
> of my hips and thighs.
>
> Yet I hear my voice rise
> as my final tear dries:
> "I'll have gravy on those fries,
> and a dozen cream pies."

Leon Rooke

SWEETHEARTS

Hey, Sweetheart, come on over. She calls me on the phone, that's what she says. Hey, Sweetheart, come on over. I say, It's late, baby, you come over here. So we argue about it. She says, But I was over there last week. I was over there last night. Wasn't I over there last night? We argue about that. I say, Was it last night? Are you sure it was last night? She says, Wait now, I could be wrong. I could be. What's your name anyhow? That's what she says: What's your name anyhow? And we argue about my name. We argue about her name. We argue about everything under the sun. She says, If you are going to argue I don't want to talk to you. I say, Talk to me. I've got to talk to someone. She says, Sweetheart, now you're talking. I'll be right over. I'll hop into a cab. Okay, I think, that settles it. She's coming. Don't get in a sweat. She'll be here pronto. Then I say, Will you spend all night? Will you? Can I count on that? And she says, Are you kidding? All night? Have you lost your senses? What about my kids? What about my toothbrush? What about all the nights I did spend all night and nothing ever happened? What about that? I say, Hold on. Hold on, I say, I think you've got the wrong party. Let's check that number again. Do we know each other? She says, If that's how you feel I'm not coming. She says, If that's how you feel you can call somebody else. I say, what I say is, Who called who? What I say is, I don't recall ringing your number. What I say is, Sweetheart, this isn't working out. She says, Whose fault is that, if I may ask you? Who started this? You always want to argue. Why do you always want to argue? You'd better get straight with yourself before you want to start making time with a woman like me. Am I making time? I say, Is that what I'm doing? I say, How much time am I making if you come over and nothing happens? She says, Did I say that? Did I? So we argue about what happens and what does not happen. We argue at considerable length about that. We are shouting into the phone and she says, Why are you shouting? Stop shouting, get a grip on yourself. But things have gone too far, I can't get a grip on myself. I can't get straight with myself. She says, I know. I know, that has always been your trouble. I say, What trouble? I wasn't in any trouble until I met you. She says, You're right. I don't doubt that for a minute. She says, I'm always trouble, I've been trouble for every man I've ever known. What I say is, No, you haven't. I say, You're a life saver, that's what you are. Thank you, she says. Thank you. It is very nice of you to say that. Even if you don't mean it, it is nice of you to say so. I mean it, I say. You've saved my life a thousand times. She says, If only I could believe that. If only we could start over. I say, Every time I see you is a new start, every time, even if nothing happens. She says, Oh God, what can I do? What can I say? When I say nothing happens I don't mean it the way you think I mean it. My head's in a whirl, that's what she says. I say, Tell me about it. She says, I can't talk now. She says, I've got to see you, what I want to say can't be said on the phone. We're in deep water, she says. How did we get in such deep water? I say, Let's talk about it. Okay, she says, okay. I'll be right over and we can talk about it, although that's all we do, is talk about it. Do you really think we should? What I say is, Yes, yes, we owe it to each other. Fine, she says, I'm on my way. Shall I pack my toothbrush? Shall I stay the night? Can we have a nice friendly dinner somewhere? The truth is I haven't eaten, I haven't eaten in days and days. I say, Same here. I say, God, I'm starving, let's do that, let's eat somewhere. She says, Good, good, I can't wait to see you. I think to myself, God, what a shot, what a woman! I can't wait to see her, that's what I think. Wear a jacket, she says, it's cold, it's very cold out there. You too, I say. Dress warmly, don't let the cold get next to your bones. She says, You know what I want next to my bones, don't you, don't you, you've always known. I say, Hurry, let's not waste any time, why have we been wasting all this time? I'm on my way, she says, I'm flying out of the door. Me, too, I say, goodbye for now. Goodbye, she says, kiss-kiss, she says, into the phone. What a woman, I think, why are you always fighting with her? No fighting, I say, anymore. Get straight with yourself, Jack, go to a nice restaurant, hold her hands, look into her eyes, get lost inside her eyes. Get inside her coat with her, run your hands over her body, warm each other, let the flesh commingle, be bone against bone, the bones in harvest, go at it breath to breath, breath with breath, forget this ashes to ashes business, just forget it. Hold her, lock eyes, get inside that coat with her. And don't stop there. Why stop there? Call the children in. Say, Children, do we have news for you! Say, Children, gather around, assemble your bedrolls, for we have important announcements to make. The world does not belong to those whom you thought it belonged to. No, it doesn't. You see this coat? Come, get inside this coat with us, let's hug each other, warm each other. Look into our eyes. Did we say "lost"? We don't mean "lost," we mean "found," as in "Eureka!" as in "Boy oh boy!" as in "new continents," "larger horizons," "greater expectations," "warmer seasons," "fabled heights," etc., you get the idea. The world doesn't belong to those you thought it belonged to, and never did. Say that, I tell myself. Tell them that. Get your act in gear. So I go down and I wait for her cab, I wait for it. She's my sweetheart, I am hers. We are sweethearts to each other, we are lovers through thick and thin. She'll be here soon, any minute now, any second now. You believe me, don't you? Accept it, every word is true. There's her cab now, turning the corner, a nice yellow one. I can see the driver, I can see her in the back seat, black coat up around her ears. Come on now, hurry, hurry it up. I want to get inside that coat with you, I want to look into your eyes, to lock hearts, to say, Cabbie, turn this cab around. Cabbie, haven't you heard the news? We've got everything, we've got all we need. What you have here, in this neighbourhood, on this freezing night, are two people, two sweethearts, who utterly desire, comprehend, and complete each other. Snow? You call this snow? This isn't snow, this isn't a freeze. We're trim and fit and ready for anything.

Stan Rogal

PERSONATIONS: 21

"How tiring it gets being the same person all the time."
— *"Hopscotch" by Julio Cortazar*

End fact. Try fiction. Let us say we see…
[Then again, don't]
A ROOM. *Any* room. Say, *this* room.
Thass a nice beginning, pal. Sound structure.
With a view, natch, of one's very own & private.
Hell. Dig? I do. I'm in it — see!
Standing at. Near the. Next to. Over by. Or (p'r'aps)
Sitting in (on?) a white/blue/yellow
Chair
Giving not half-assed *serious* consideration:
   why time don't tick to the beat of a heart
Unnatural.

Meanwhile, t/here is a window where a window would normal
Be. Outside this, a deck. On the deck, aligned
 in some set (& particular) sweet manner:
    planters, plants, a right
    solid varnished wood table
    & gas *bar-b-cue*.
What is common called "a middle-classed arrangement."

Beyond the deck, the trees. Beyond the trees, the tracks.
Beyond the tracks, the factories. Beyond the factories…
You go too far already, suh. You exceed the limits.

108 Carnival

Adder exacts a toll, yes, & vice functions as it will, but,
Birds? Weather? A fertile plot?
Inevitably. Though these are nowhere near the same.
As "a murder of crows" looses its grip with overuse.
Or "a dark and stormy night"
    or "a garden of earthly delights"
Finally
Up & withers.
What came before has served & must needs be renewed.

                    And then went down to the ship.
[Then again, don't] Didn't.   Only remains
For what good reason, who knows?
Here (repeat) is the room I keep forgetting (or, is it
I can't remember).
Remains of an animal roast in the oven.
Remains of an animal roast in the oven because, I say:
    "Remains of an animal... etc."
A glass of red/white wine upon the plain
Chequered cloth. Butts in the ashtray.
An unlit match.
An untried apple.
You fear from hunger, no? So, awright, *give.*
Still life after all. After all the.
Sacrifice. Petals, &, whatever else, image.
"Heart to heart," they say. "Heart to earth," is more
Likely, as: this was *likely* the case that such-&-such.

                    And then went down to the ship.
[Then again, don't] This being Sunday, a fifth of March
Nineteen hundred & ninety-three in the year of our lord.
Christ! The way snow steady blasts the afternoon &
History doth loud decant: O, POUND IS DEAD!
Thass a sad ole fac', Jack. What boots?
What boots is I am just as well
    (having today turned forty-three)
Remains
Now&forever

Tick

Dark Horses

Moving one orbit to another
    w/o benefit of middle ground
        punches holes in a well-formed plain
    that images sequential.
Here is an example of the single fine Art.

    (THE FIRST OF 3 IN A ROW)

Devoid of any reasonable residue
    or any other excess, save,
This rider.
Unlike trying to go beyond the crowd from within.
Sure as shit.
Nothing works in this hell that requires a Phillips
    while you're still stripping screws
        with a fucking flathead.
No as-if but truly:

        American media continues to love
        what it cannot possess
        & kill what it cannot love.

Romancing the dark horse, always,
    with technology enuf to put cleavage on a rattlesnake
Forsakes the Real.
Forsook.
Devotion falling back on a strip of film that proved
    4 feet off the ground &
        rendered every frame worth remarking.
Now bored clear thru at the edges. Lost.
Mystery thumbing its nose at the finish.
No way to treat a public that appreciates:

sounds pulled by a finger
from the rim
of a glass
is not music
until
someone
calls it
Music.

Business being (typically)
    once you're in, you're out
        a Carpenter
            fades from the picture
                except as
Image.
The perfect pitch driving the perfect vehicle.
Recognizing all bets favour the dead.
This we call religion.

> (THE SECOND OF 3 IN A ROW
> BARELY BREAKS A SWEAT)

Content to make do with the only maps available
        eschatology buries its nose dangerously near the sphincter
            immortality harnessed to the re-turning of old ground
                & the empty claim:

> "Miracles present themselves
> Constantly
> To the prepared mind."

Yet, (not believing for an instant
            this track ain't as crooked as the rest)
Picks the long shot & loses by a mile.

> (THE THIRD OF 3 IN A ROW)

Tricia Postle

TODAY I'M GOING TO BE A MAN

Today, I'm going to be a man.
I'm going to wear black clothes
And no makeup.
OK.   No difference.
But it's inside
I'm wearing black clothes
And no makeup
And I won't think
That I'd look better with eyeliner.
Today, I'm a man.
I'm not going to wear any fitted clothing.
If someone wants
To know that I have breasts,
They're going to have to look.
I'm wearing a black suit jacket.
I'm a man.

Today, I'm going to be a man.
I have short hair, and a
Black suit jacket, and
I'm six feet tall;
Today, I'm a man.
I'm saying just what's on my mind,
Even if it's not much.
I'm a man!

Today, I'm going to be a man;
I'll objectify you if you don't mind.
I feel insecure, tra la,
Today, I'm a man.
I'll go off and invade a small country,
And no one will make any
Comments about the size of my penis.
I'm a man.

Today, I'm going to be a man;
I know what wines to order
I have good teeth! I'm a man!
I'm here! I'm large!
I like scotch and soda!

Women look at my finely boned hands, and swoon!
I protect the city from undesirables!
I own a really nice revolver!
I practice shooting
Imaginary diamond thieves over my desk!
I go to clubs and pick up cute young blonde women who giggle!
I'm a lawyer, I think!
Or am I a junior partner in my father's firm?
Or did I start my own software company
As a boy genius at eighteen, which now
Has subsidiary branches in New York, L.A.,
Munich, Paris and Berlin?
It's so hard to remember.

I'm a man today!
I'm so charming
You may want to hit me.
I have great cheekbones.
I'm sensitive, too,
I mean, overlooking that
Time I invaded the small country,
So they wouldn't think, you know...
But no, really,
I care about the environment, and things like that,
And I think it's important that
We all start paying attention to the world
Around us.
I love you.
Really.
You're one of the most caring,
Open women that I've ever met.
There's something about you
That's so... so honest.
I worry about you, you know.
When you're not with me.
Let me see you home.
Waiter!
Thank you.
Ah.
When the light hits you like that, it's magical.
I don't want to keep you up too late...
No, that's fine, the weather's perfect
It's only a short walk,
Well then, as long as you tell me when you want me to leave...
You don't have to be kind if you don't want to...
Lewis Carroll!
Yes!
I'm a huge fan!
Oh, I want to kiss you!
You're so beautiful.
Yes!
Yes!
YES!
YES!

114 Carnival

Yes, today I'm a man.
I weep openly at the ballet!
I'm involved in regional politics!
I get money for grants, and scoff openly
At Reform party toadies
Who call me a special interest group!
I know good restaurants!
I explain how women really think to unhappy male friends!
I rush through the streets like a wild boar in the thickets,
Pink, prickly, tailored, and debonair,
Singing hoarsely to the four winds.
I'm a man, yes;
Today, I am a man!

COMMENTARY

This poem is going to be
Short.

Clifton Joseph

(I REMEMBER) BACK HOME

i remember back home
& the promise of young/fun
crickets/crackling,
orange sun's east/glance
when the day is done: i remember back home back home back home

i remember short/pants
& cricket/balls........... rolling a/long
picnics & motor/cades,
politics & rum.
i remember back home
& the promise of young/fun:
marbles,
grundoves,
elbows running mango juice,
donkey trots of thoughts,
fresh/baked spiced/buns, i remember
back home, back home, back home:

116 Carnival

i remember steel/band's bright/blue blast/of/joy
the heart's tropical patter/like loud, coloured/columns of West
African/drums
i remember bloomed/bougainvillea braggingly
/swaying in the sandy wind, i remember
back home,
back home,
back home:
i remember back/home
& sweeping the yard
carrying water/on/heads on roads/of/marl,
detentions/lines/writings &/teacher's/beatings/real-hard
i remember back home...
& it wasn't all good:
four/to/a/bed
& some nights without food
it wasn't all bright smiles
sea/sand/sun/&/fun,
back home had its share
of oppression in the sun,
back home has its share
of dreams burnt in the sun,
dreams burnt in the sun
dreams burnt in the sun.

i remember back home
& the promise of young/fun:
fish/frys, tea-parties & endless chatter
dominoes/clatter at cutlass/slammer
slow hand/claps as boundaries/shatter
cricketers running in the rain, in the thunder
crowds/shout-out syncopated/laughter
politicians/get/rich the/people/don't/matter
progress/gets/lost in/the/trail of/the/dollar
oppression/handed/down from/mother/to/brother...
back/home, back home
back home gots/to get better.

R.M. Vaughan

REQUIEM FROM A HEADY HEIGHT
from THE MULLIN TRILOGY

a sick room, familiar to anyone who knows about opera or the nineteenth century

that shirt, the colour of hankies
    a double breast of bent cotton
    boiled to kill mites and flat-ironed
to hold you together

— we have to pay mind to so many things
    … the way the carpet curls under the floorboards
like a tongue
    too smooth for dust and tight as hospital corners

a symbol of eternity, it should remind the reader of headstones

the barest window sill, cut in thirds by the sun
holds:
three wooden boxes, nothing inside;
some twists of eucalyptus, dried whip stiff;

one eye-shaped stone
salty to the palm

118 Carnival

a room consciously empty, as if your body needed all the attention

and you taking the farthest corner, out of earshot
(and long habit)   and to see better
the nerve architects have to call a skyline fluid

the vulgar history of building on top of building

the wind reminds me only an inch of winter-hardened glass
is everything between you and the evidence of everything
under the sun   past you, already

blinds could blunt this metaphor
faster than your death   only
hold onto me and
shut up   I'm not the one so sure I'll land
on my feet

in which I offer a humble criticism

this is the kind of place men who fear for their lives live in
— simply a built-up burrow   the damn thing puts mice   to shame—
your scooped out resting place, lined with paper, old clothes,
tired ideas about death

…you see   he thinks his Table of Elements
that broken scrabble of syllables I used to know by heart
is growing
and this upsets him, as everything unchecked does

this is the sort of place men scared of death decorate
cover with   irony-free curtains   (the   dying have an interest in
quality fabrics, considering burials)
accent with hopeless potted plants, stacks of coffee cups (why
clean now?) and saucers, ringed at the bottom like chopped trees

this is the type of fated man to whom another hour
means nothing   morning is a précis, a worn symbol of innocence
he's the easiest type to kill, smother with a pillow
'cause another hour means pushing half (or more)   the day's work
of breathing, eating, shitting,   into tomorrow
where   another noonday is a healthy man's idea
of a deadline

because death is more plausible in the evening, for obvious reasons

he re-arranges the dark hours   peels each fingernail
down to the underwhite   keeps the night's piss inside
knots tight a bed scarf   sits on the hard of his knees
  — all old soldiers' spells to stay alert

... funny   them not working in reverse
     in daylight   because death is a nice idea
     in a busy world
     there are counter-tricks for dying   in his sleep:
get up, untie the sheets
lie flat, like a monk
align the body North/South, with the poles
read a dull book   swallow something

the question of tears arose

in a bungalow close to the ground
a phone call, blunt as a bedroom curtain
  another signal from strangers

but you've been dead before
  in three dreams (that I remember)
· half a dozen poems   every chance look at the out of town papers
your death has never been less than just ahead

you were not famous   I could make you so

a summing up betraying the conceit of intimacy

I could believe in Love if I didn't fall into it every day

or a planned death, a demise set to scale
the heights of these buildings   to the quiet, higher air
to cut me to a slow crawl   to the top   and then to nothing

I'll say it I don't think you earned your death
as hard as you could
      be angry at words like victim, patient, client
                at a city run by disappointed children
      at a dumbing hour's nap, taken by accident
you never screamed   in front of me
called out to God
pulled a single hair
      rage thrown to the air   up here   only whistles

who gets my letters?
or the handful of snow-banded amethyst (healing rocks, best
thrown away now)
or   the turkish box, a hectagon of resin and gold-pricked
vellum   so easily stained by newspaper packing
            all those books?

thumbing her way down my love letters   can your mother imagine
my face? can she make the leap from mattress   to mailbox   to
mattress again (and then never again)
to a day bed and flowers and no sharp words   ever again

a leap as tall as this, your last and tallest building

SCREAM IN HIGH PARK
A Carnival of the Spoken Word

Monday, July 19th, 1993
7pm 'til midnight

rain date: July 26th

A Multimedia performance of poetry and fiction on the set of the Canadian Stage Company's "Dream in High Park" featuring...

SET ONE (7-8pm)
Adeena Karasick
Yves Troendle
Lea Harper
Roo Borson

SET TWO (8-9pm)
Christopher Dewdney
Steven Heighton
Barbara Gowdy
Peter McPhee
& His Uneven Rhythm

SET THREE (9-10pm)
Christine Slater
Micheal Holmes
Christian Bök
Paul Dutton

SET FOUR (10-11pm)
Sky Gilbert
David Donnell
Lynn Crosbie
bill bissett

come early (around 5pm)
bring a picnic!
bring a friend!
suggested donation -- $5

for more information contact:
Matthew Remski, Artistic Director, 534-0987

MONDAY, JULY 19, 1993
ATTENDANCE: 450
ARTISTIC DIRECTOR: MATTHEW REMSKI

Yves Troendle

DEAD GIVEAWAY (RE: ROBERT RAUSCHENBERG)

Leave the base and get on Highway 101. Go to the Palladium.
Watch your step. Walk ten miles. Talk to a piece of tin. Say things like,
"I don't want to know who did this." Show your usual good judgement.
Ask to be called Dada. Be stranger than fiction. Use contradiction.
Don't blame mom.
Just go on painting. Neutralize.

Do these simple everyday things. Honour the Swedish. Sit in a house.
Look at the glass. Fabricate. Take a handful. Clear the way.
Dance with women. Be a princess. Tell the difference. Keep changing.
Rely on immediate sight. Think of the souvenirs without nostalgia.
Spend the night on the highway. Bring back the reality of the surface.
Erase.

Work flat for a while. Know what you mean by realistic.
Have nothing to lose. Pick up cardboard boxes. Paint on them. Really need.
Be elitist. Think Matisse. Get really simple.
Help me break the rest of these up.

Get out of Port Arthur. Get away to think. Just learn to swim.
Be dressed in white. Push something that doesn't have a centre. Keep it going.
Leave the gallery. Get serious. Bring in Etruscan things
and occasionally a marble bust. Just ramble on so beautifully.
Stop the wall. Ask me over. Read Marshall McLuhan to me.
Keep the windows open.

Shut down the whole relationship.
Keep the television on all the time.
Go to a party, have a drink, say excuse me,
and be back in forty-five seconds.

Show me the town. Double the space. Make for the unexpected.
Don't go without a jar. Think performance. Bring the room. Change it.
Take images from any source. Look as little like a particular point of view
as possible.

Change the scene. Erase art. Open up. Use chance. Change time.
Use about fifteen different types of erasers.
Be the room itself.

Come in. Have a concept. Remember the day. Have a copy.
Never forget it. Stop me from falling in love with it. Focus on the rock.
Be something else. Have one of the weirdest careers in the Navy. Swim.
Go through the jungle. Run by the state. Add up to something.
Paint "de Kooning" all the time. Tell shit from Shinola.
Mean that as a compliment. Produce extraordinary changes in the world.
Do or say. Win or lose. Get out of bed right on time, hollering.

Wake up every morning. Paint with my hands. Ennoble the ordinary.
Go right out of it. Run out of clothes. Discover perspective.
Get the proper help. Ring for service. Make decisions — weird ones — instantly.

Cover the walls. Look out the window. Be my appetite. Never even blink.
Absorb whatever images appear in the room. Diagnose the whole thing
over the telephone. Get more exaggerated. Read one instant.
Go out in the middle of Union Square. Look like anything. Match the environment.
Swim through my brain. Keep the fan on. Go out looking.
Move consciously in one direction. Walk across the United States
and photograph it foot by foot in actual size. Risk performing.
Call me back. Eclipse our differences. Amuse myself.
Feel invisible. Get close to that camera. Be there when I'm gone.
Put up the pieces, one at a time. Burn.

Happen very naturally. Look okay in a gallery. Look like trash. Make up your mind.
Go swimming in it. Scream in the audience. Head for the sun.
Have a different thought. Keep the questions changing.
Have time to teach the dancers. Have a gorgeous chrysanthemum.
Have a couple of photos of it. Have a feeling. Have a good time turning.
Have three. Have two days off. Have less. Have one.
Have the same problem all the time.

Leave this marvellous woman. Stop coming to class. Object to the subject.
Move away from the black and white. Walk a tightrope on the floor.
Be the first one to see. Have the only jungle left. Break up and go crazy.
Talk about art. Come in and talk for thirty-six hours straight.
Be labelled great. Go through everybody's garbage.
Think. Okay, he's asleep. Do the Inferno.
Be monochrome.

Support the structure of growing plants. Protest against the bourgeoisie.
Run out of things to paint on. Smear it on. Rope it off. Make no discrimination.
Stop a line, say, at the ear. Assume precisely what it is we should be questioning.
Be academic. Be a show. Pass like fashion. Be quite an interesting disaster.
Doodle all the time. Do a one-man tango. Burst into tears.
Realize it isn't me. Spend the rest of my life working with dancers.

Avoid my habits. Keep everything going.
Avoid turtles crossing the road. Carry out my end of the bargain.
Be the one to pick her up. Stop off in Los Angeles. Turn off the ignition.
Take a little chewing gum and stick. Illustrate that this must be the case.
Wait a long time in a coffee shop. Look around. Look inevitable.
Document what's going on in a room. Visualize a box. Call up and
talk your way out. Come up with about five hundred new ideas.
Address the United Nations with our intentions. Move to another planet.

Move in and out of space. Drive them crazy. Eat lunch. Give up art.
Be in danger. Look.

Adeena Karasick

FLORUIT RETINUE

I

And before the sun, walls,
windows. Before
sequences opulence in the virus of
trellis suffices,

diurnal linen lineament
ciphers in the fullness like
a metonymic mimic

in the definition of
difference, appliance,
appearance

II

In Lilongwe. Takin' la langue way. plus de
langue, lingers. As her tongue. kiss*. mouth.
closed around ellipse slip. tasting the tongue of
a tongue, a tome. L'anglais en Lilongwe. No
lily-livered sasaparilla suckin' swill way. sways
as her tongue, teeth, lips part, solypse sip in
prolixis licks; a ventrilosquist kiss. in the
darkness of slick kissery articulate, as accessory
synnexes in the nexus collapses into
meconnaises kenosis kinesis askance.

Lilongwe, le *langelait*. In the intimacy of bor-
ders, tongue.lick.taste. As clavicle hollow
slack ex-schize kiss caught in the covets risks
limits lip clots distance with desire

ou est Lilongwe, l'angue way.

III

As linguae grinds
in the magnate of rhetorical invasion.

IV

A ravenous graft
or traumatic masque acts
returns/upon itself
in the midday difference
in the horror of desire

(ne pas de horror) or
abhoria or

in anamnesis,
mnemesis

unheimlich ich:

---

*You must remember this.
A kiss is still a kiss. (As Time Goes By)

130 Carnival

V

In the sting of
abdicate covets incurs
in splenetic extension

her supplicant cunning
surfaces in yr cumulus
down. In the matrix of resistance
insistence. Her reticent
dissensus resents

that maybe
hot and steamy maybe

VI

'cause interstitially speaking,
a misspelled swill of
kichotic crops
in the comma of
request. In the
famine laminate
latrine hydrax jacks,

but the river was wide and i swam it,
'cause damn it, i am it, and i love

when you hunker down
in the genre of

slipstream sucking light
come flummery

in the alliance of
night screws, clamps,
stains, questions,
as if i care in the gnawing
in the envy,

in a surplus of
spectrality, sacrality, alterity
syncretic etiquette
acts in the risk of
fixity [sic]
exits in

VII

yr look or locus
acted out in

> the echo of
> articulation
> in the stain of
> resistence splits

And i hear yr hearing

folds or
faint feign
focusses/fixed as

the reminder or
remainder

> in the economy of a foci loci
> skewhiff riff, as if
> stiffed as an ambient
> pamby sifted in

VIII

insinuant sinews solypse. as a threnody already.
an anachronistic massacre or an aneurysm mannerism

before.
exordium mortem or

Christopher Dewdney

THE CLOUDS

Barrie Nichol died in the autumn of 1988. For several weeks afterward the weather was unusually constant. Each afternoon large cumulus clouds mounted east of the city while, at the same time, a high, grey, uniform cloud-cover, thin enough to show the disk of the sun, spread over the sky. This layer of cloud subdued the light cast on the eastern cumulus banks and steeped their topography in a cool, grey summer light. The daily constancy of the clouds made each afternoon preternaturally similar, as if time had stopped and the same day was being replayed again and again.

These afternoons, with their neutral temperature, resonated in the absence Barrie's death had created. The unearthly permanence of the cloud banks made it seem that a new mountain range had risen east of the city. And yet, because all this structure and complexity was only water vapour in the atmosphere, floating islands sculpted by gravity and convection currents, the cloud banks became a paradigm of our own condition. We were like the clouds, sublime, marvellously detailed and ethereal all at once, mere convolutions of form with no permanence or substance. We were, as was everything around us, involutions of time and space. The world was a lucid, exquisitely complex, heartbreakingly beautiful, sad and strange illusion.

To awaken, dream, and then sleep again. We are thinking clouds.

THE FOSSIL FOREST OF AXEL HEIBERG

Some forty-five million years ago, the earth's climate was so mild that the Arctic regions had a subtropical climate. Axel Heiberg, a large island in the Canadian Arctic, was the site of a lush forest of dawn redwoods and palmettos. It is thought that deciduous trees first acquired their habit of shedding their leaves in these Eocene Arctic forests, for summer nights lasted five months.

The Arctic Eocene forest rises from the floor of a vast, dark library. The deserted wing of a Georgian museum. Its ceiling beams cannot be seen above the stars, nor its walls beyond the horizon. During the still months of the Arctic night, meteoric dust falls from the sky. It powders the leaves of the forest like the leaves of untended lobby plants in a vacant apartment building. On the forest floor pastel shadows flicker under the aurora borealis.

Lemurs slip through the stillness — silent, quick hallucinations. Their claws rustle on the ribboned bark of the dawn redwoods. They are the only movement in this inconceivable atrium, this subtropical, polar forest of perpetual twilight.

The Eocene Arctic forest is a hiatus in time where abandoned lovers return to each other. It is where secrets are kept, a lonely place of solitary wandering. It is the arena of love gone vacant, of heartbroken lovers deserted by mad partners. A zone of silent, strange encounters — luminescent mushroom gardens fluttering with giant tropical moths. And when the wind comes, soft at first, then rushing, spreading through the night forest, the first chords of the great Nachtmusik are written.

And the chill rain, sometimes for weeks.

134 Carnival

We are waiting
at the line between
today and tomorrow, night
and day. The planetary
terminator line, stalled
in perpetual twilight
early in the Arctic Eocene night.

In the continuous flux of the world,
in its debris, I pronounce the ritual names.
The Eocene terminator line
holds us in its dusky thrall
as the mists of a forty-million-
year-old forest
rise again to the canopy.

VIGILANCE

I am a sensualist, attenuated by constant vigilance.

•

Music adds an unnatural glory to our lives.

•

Language was given to us by aliens, as a tool.

•

Only the adjectives have been changed to protect the names of the innocent.

•

If I were in your shoes you'd be wearing size nine.

•

The future is simply amnesia in reverse.

Roo Borson

SUMMER CLOUD

Hello little buntings, if that's what you are —
you look as though you should be reading the stock reports,
keeping up your options on soybeans, gold, and millet.
I married a man once who said the strangest things.
Years later at an airport he knelt down to pray
and the Playboy magazines spilled out of his briefcase.
How is it people can go on to become anything at all?
The incomprehensible crystals in the government vault
by which we measure space and time.
The body is impossible. You can hack off every limb
and still it goes on thinking it's whole. It dies,
only to feel it's walking around fully dressed.
Are you in the forest?
One day the grass turns green, and all
the merry little bands of boys
call out to one another in the high, gruff,
sulky voices of robber kings. And no wonder.
This world is only a template for the world,
all painted with a whitewash called Summer Cloud.

THE LIMITS OF KNOWLEDGE, TILTON SCHOOL, NEW HAMPSHIRE

At certain points in the universe longing condenses,
the shade sucked against the screen,
the plain dishevelled ruffles that frame
the window — because a girl sleeps here during the year,
a school, a desk, the simple chair whose
duty and forgiveness are the weight of all matter.
A month from now someone's daughter
will enter this room,
her hair will fall along her back,
she will sit in struggle with
thoughts not her own, the books in front of her,
hour after hour — medieval really,
this illimitable patience, as at the bedside
of the dying, whom one loves —
and how the skin and breasts are lit by faint
sensations, that which asks as well
for knowledge *through* another.
What can be discovered within four walls?
Walls a pale green found nowhere in
nature but in the wings of a rare
moth that startled me once,
near, as big as my hand,
and whose colouration
mimics it.
Let us call it
learning, redisposing oneself, hour after hour,
to be as one is urged, cajoled,
told. I have lived in this room,
made love here, the man sleeps beside me.
Will she sense our trespass as an opening?
Or will she, like the local girl who served our dinner,
a few dollars and a summer job with which to
dabble in freedom,
think this town ugly,
because that is how she sees her life so far,
and she has not lived elsewhere.

Steven Heighton

Nakunaru

In the Japanese language *to die*
is to become invisible, to be lost
to go missing
                    so when Hideyuki Murata disappeared
in the August blast, scoured
from a street in the core of Nagasaki
                    haunting the upper air as atoms of heat
or energy mingled with cinders
                    of his wife and children winnowing
down into fields along the coast
                                        •

                    So when he disappeared, it seemed
his language had already prepared
a vocabulary to deal with his loss
                    and when Hideyuki went
with his 75 years, he took
these things with him: •

                    the peculiar bluegreen
his eyes made of bays east of Shimabara
when he first fished there with his uncle
                    the way the paddy-field by his house
had smelled in the summer heat, of rice
steaming, newly cooked
his mother's voice calling him to supper
                    a freak snow one April, melted down

138 Carnival

by noon, the sweet
stab of a crabapple
biting into his tongue, a best friend shot beside him
at Mukden, 1905
his first monsoon his father dead
and a woman kissed him —

                and old eyes noting in wind
over the harbour
a single silver gleam — a seagull maybe
flying inland, catching the early light

and disappearing
with a clap of thunder
into remarkable clouds

THE ECSTASY OF SKEPTICS

EXIT signs in the scholars' hallway
Lead through polished sheets of plate glass
Into air into thin air —

                          outborne
From an ivory silence
Where the world was to be rephrased
Where the skeleton key of learned
Rigour, cracks
Feckless in the lock, where screens
Glow green as chlorophyll (or
Landfill, breeding—a Babel
Of cavilled, rootless words that mean,
In the heart's hearing, what?)

                          This tongue
is a moment of moistened dust, it must learn
to turn the grit of old books
into hydrogen, and burn
The dust of the muscles must burn
down the blood-fuse of the sinews, the tendons'
taut wick, these bones like tinder giving light
to read by, and heat, the winter light is already
lagging, we'll soon be less than cinders, adrift
in an aftermath of space...

Voices in the scholars' hallway
lead through fastened doors
into catacombs of jargon, parchment hives.

Now, love. This way. With the lights on. Blazing.

Peter McPhee

WHY THE STEGOSAURUS IS MY FAVOURITE DINOSAUR

A small boy is walking backwards in the rain
humming a music
        disconnected from notes I might string together
late for school
oblivious to everything
but the pauses in his song.

Yesterday
leaves slipped on the wind.
Matted they cling to the red-brick heels
of black rubber boots
and hold on desperately
for any hope a boy can give.

With careful steps
he turns
avoids cracks, worms and weeds
until the plastic of his hat is lifted in the air
        spinning him again.

On the uneven sidewalk
he scrapes summer from his sole.

He believes in dinosaurs.
Not only that they once roamed freely
        (as cats between fenceposts)
but that they still live
                fiercely
in schoolyards
        and sleep.

He's seen the footprints
and will show you
if you let him.

Great herds of terrible horns and teeth
breaking trails to the wonder of
where they are in the day.

Extinct
his father says.

Imagine Stegosaurus:

a walnut brain
steering the bulk of an elephant

ancient and awkward herds
circling to protect the young

not an exact science

a herbivore
a relative of birds

the power and balance
of a long spiked tail

intrigue
a protruding plate
solar attraction to the cold-blooded morning

the ugly likeliness
                    of its expression.

---

142 Carnival

Consider a conversation with myself
mumbling on about the mesozoic
the rise of flowering plants
the death of the dinosaur.

Balance your diet.
Eat a vegetarian.
65 million years
the only wisdom for carnivores
and not an acceptable answer.

Someone says
Not this Monday
but Monday next…
and I wait
through an ice-age
and a drought

and no one says
The dinosaur
lovely as the world's first flower
and I am aware of more than emptiness
or the want of fallen lovers.

I see the sound of the pause
in a child's hummed notes
the invisible
beginning in the lungs
and fading with the sunset

bewildered under stars
I blunder backwards through millennia
and know only the magic
of believing the impossible.

The rain stops

              for the last time maybe.
The wind
singing a wrong and difficult key
leaves museum skeletons
bleached and marrowless branches
peeled bark
the discovery of fire

the wind
a spiral in the corner of a schoolyard
a challenge to the freedom of leaves.

Why is the Stegosaurus my favourite dinosaur?

Watching a small boy
                  late and in no hurry
I am lost in a lifetime of ages
and I know
it has something to do
with the danger
of the tail.

Barbara Gowdy

RESURRECTION (1969)

All three girls are in the front seat. The fat girl with the glasses is driving. In the back seat their father is asleep sitting up.

They pull into the parking lot, and two men who are leaning against a blue Volkswagen van turn to look at them. One of the men has a camera round his neck. "Fuck," the thin girl says.

Their father jerks awake. Before the car has come to a full stop, he has his door open. "Scram!" he yells at the men. He falls out the door, onto one knee. The three girls quickly get out of the car. Their father stands up and heads for the men, thrashing his arms. "Vamoose!" he yells. "Bugger off!" The men don't move.

"Dad," the fat girl pleads. Their father staggers away from everyone and slaps his pockets for cigarettes.

"Just leave him," the thin girl mutters. She starts walking, giving their father a wide berth. Her sisters follow. The fat girl with the glasses can't squeeze between the fenders of the two hearses, and she reddens, conscious of the men approaching. "Climb over," the thin girl orders. Glancing at the photographer, she reaches into her purse and gets out the pack of cigarettes that their father is searching for. If she has to have her picture taken, she wants to be smoking.

The photographer starts clicking. But not at the thin girl. He aims at the third girl, the pretty blonde one, who is waiting while the fat sister climbs over the fenders. "Figures," the thin girl thinks. The pretty girl gazes at the scorched white sky as if wondering whether their mother is up there yet.

"Excuse me," the second man says, sauntering up. The pretty girl smiles politely. The thin girl narrows her eyes. The eyes of the man are rabid with fake pity. He says it's a real drag about their mother and he hates like hell to hassle them, but the pictures aren't going to have captions unless he gets their names straight.

Both the fat girl and the pretty one look at the thin girl. "Lou," the thin girl says. The man flips open a pad and starts writing. Lou nods at the fat girl, "Norma," nods at the pretty girl, "Sandy." This is the first reporter that Lou's let anywhere near her. It's because he has long hair and a beard and is wearing blue jeans.

"Still in high school?" the reporter asks conversationally.

"For another few weeks, yeah." Lou blows a smoke ring. The photographer goes on clicking at Sandy.

"When did you get the cat?" the reporter asks.

"What?"

"The cat. Your mother went up on the roof to rescue a cat, didn't she?"

"We better get inside," Norma murmurs.

Sweat starts dripping down the reporter's forehead. "I understand that one of you was there when it happened," he says, earnest now.

"We were all there," Lou says. Her hand shakes bringing her cigarette up to her mouth. "Okay, we've got to go," she says, moving around the reporter, feeling herself on a dangerous verge.

Inside the funeral parlour, Sandy asks where the washroom is. She has decided to put her false eyelashes back on.

It's not vanity, like Lou thinks. This morning Lou said, "You've got too much makeup on. Nobody'll believe you're broken up." So Sandy took her eyelashes off, but now she wishes she hadn't, and not only because of the photographer. She can't understand why someone as smart as Lou hasn't figured out that the better you look, the better people treat you.

She bats her lashes to see if they're stuck on. "Beauty is only skin deep," she tells herself defensively. She has always taken this expression to mean that only what is skin deep is beautiful.

Her throat tightens. She has had an awful thought. In an autopsy they remove all your organs, don't they? She isn't sure. But just the idea of strange men rummaging around inside their mother... She thinks of their mother's organs sloshing in whiskey. She thinks of their mother's womb, and she starts crying and fishes in her purse for Kleenex. Even before their mother died, the depressing image of her womb crossed Sandy's mind a couple of times. She pictured an empty draw-string purse.

146 Carnival

Norma and Lou go into the room where their mother is. Nobody else has arrived yet. They're an hour early because yesterday their aunt phoned and told them to be. The casket is against the far wall, between big green plants that you can tell from the door are plastic.

Norma walks over. "Is she all here?" she whispers. Only the upper part of the casket is open, and the lower part doesn't seem long enough.

"Who gives a shit," Lou says in a steady voice. "She's dead." Last night Lou cried her heart out. Their sweet little mother who tap-danced… have they cut off her legs? No way is Lou going to look in the casket.

She walks to the window and parts the heavy velvet drapes. Their father is yelling at the newspapermen again. They are about ten yards away from him, standing their ground. Lou can't hear their father, but the newspapermen are nodding as if whatever he's yelling makes a lot of sense.

Norma touches the tip of their mother's small nose. "It's me," she whispers. Their mother's nose is like a pebble, cool. Her face is white and smooth as a sink, and Norma realizes it's because the blood has been drained from her. "What do they do with the blood?" she asks Lou.

"Christ," Lou says, lighting another Export A. "Do you *mind*?" She wonders if Sandy went to the washroom to cry. In a couple of weeks Sandy plans to marry a guy who has the stupidest face Lou has ever seen on a person not mongoloid retarded. Lou suddenly has a panicky feeling that she has to put a stop to the wedding. As soon as possible. Today.

She closes her eyes. What the hell is going on? she asks herself. What does she care who Sandy marries? Maybe their mother is seeping out, and Lou has swallowed Maternal Instinct. People in Wales believe that you can swallow a dead person's sin. But their mother had no sin, and nobody can tell Lou that she sure had *one*, the biggest one, because Lou has always viewed that as a sacrifice. Their mother had no instincts left either, now that Lou thinks about it. Drowning pain Lou doesn't count.

When Lou opens her eyes, Sandy is entering the room on the arm of an undertaker. He gestures toward the casket, disengages himself and backs away, and pressing her hands at her mouth, Sandy walks over and stands beside Norma.

"She's got lipstick on," Sandy says.

"They always do that," Norma says.

"But she never wore pink lipstick," Sandy says, her voice breaking. She slowly brings her hand down and touches her fingers to their mother's lips. "Are her insides in her?" she asks.

"I think so."

"They're pickled in formaldehyde," Lou says. Lou is still looking out the window. Their father has just accepted a flask from the reporter, and now he's shaking the reporter's hand. "What a prick," Lou says.

Norma sighs. She walks over to a chair and drops into it and removes her glasses, which have felt too tight ever since they fell into the eavestrough. She knows that the prick Lou is referring to isn't one of the newspapermen, it's their father. Lou says she hates their father. Norma's never been able to hate him and especially couldn't now, when he's so pathetic. Even Lou has to admit that he loved their mother. What drove their mother to drink and probably to the roof, and what drove him, part way at least, to every bad, crazy thing he did, never really drove the two of them apart. Yesterday, in their mother's bedside table, Norma found the kidney stone that he gave their mother — for luck and instead of an engagement ring — on the night they met. Lou wouldn't look at it. Lou blames him.

Lou turns from the window. Norma is staring at her without glasses. Sandy is crying quietly, leaning into the casket. She seems to be stroking their mother's face.

"What are you doing?" Lou asks her.

"Changing her lipstick," Sandy sobs.

Lou feels nauseated. "I need some air," she says and leaves the room.

Going around a corner in the hall, she bumps into their father.

"Oh, hi!" he says, astonished.

His whiskey breath makes her stomach heave. "The last room on the left," she says, shoving by him.

She opens an Exit door and is in the parking lot. The heat slams into her. The photographer is gone, but the reporter is still there, resting against a car that's in the shade. He gets up and wanders over.

"What are you hanging around for?" she asks.

"Waiting for you." He lights her cigarette. The back of his hands and forearms have a rug of black hair on them. "So," he says, "was it an accident or what?"

"Didn't the whiskey loosen my father's tongue?" she asks sarcastically.

"I'd like to hear what you've got to say."

She wonders why she doesn't tell him. It's none of his business, but that's not the reason.

"Off the record," he says. "Strictly between you and I."

"Between you and *me*," she corrects him.

He dips his head to look in her face. He has whiskey breath, too.

"I've got to go back in," she says, tossing away most of her cigarette.

"Hey, come on." He grabs her arm.

"Let go."

"One minute, okay?"

"FUCK OFF, OKAY?"

They stare at each other. He drops his hand.

In the washroom she looks for feet under the cubicle doors. Sees none. She shuts herself in a cubicle and starts crying. She can't believe it, it makes her mad, because last night she imagined she experienced the final evolution of her heart.

What is she crying about? Not about their mother or about the baby that she cried at the thought of having and still wouldn't keep. She isn't crying for these deaths on either side of her.

She's crying because... She doesn't know why. But when she's cried herself out, the relief leaves her light-headed. No, it's more than relief — it's the same feeling she had up on the roof with their mother and Norma (although she never felt more separate from everyone), when she was above the whole subdivision, and the clouds rolling from horizon to horizon made her think of a great migration. The wind whipped her hair. It was warm and windy. Not dark or light. Their father couldn't get to her. He couldn't climb the ladder! Their mother wouldn't climb down. There was a standoff, a stopping of time. Something was going to happen — Lou felt that much, although she didn't know it was going to be something so terrible — but in that suspended minute or two, Lou was in heaven, on the verge of flying even. Doing out of no fear what their mother, a few seconds later, did terrified.

michael holmes

from 21 HOTELS

> *We keep coming back and coming back*
> *To the real: to the hotel instead of the hymns*
> *That fall upon it out of the wind.*
> — *Wallace Stevens*

THE CHESTNUT

Aesculi. The piercer's trepan augurs pikemen with sutures. Precision of miniature excavation and smooth insertion. Any flaw in the hard outer shell promotes tectonic faults, compromising the circumference. A scorched needle sucks flesh upon itself as it transudes, creating a vacuum around menacing crimson thread. The knots are not immaterial, they must buffer both point of entry and exit wound. Cure with wine vinegar. Every teen, aged and weathered by climacteric extremes and self-mutilation, makes this prosthetic stronger. Ruthless aggression pits memory against its antithesis. History sears in absolution, the heart's penance. Memory must conquer memory or be enslaved, forgotten. Only now do I remember the games I played as a child. They are this game: abnegation and flight, wanderlust, destruction.

BOB CRANE

In your penultimate role as special guest pediatrician to Jack Klugman's *Quincy* you exchanged your purple heart for a labcoat and the sybilline language of forensics. Although in this anomalous episode the ME himself, never appears. (An Asian pathologist, not Sam the sidekick or even Pat Morita, has more lines.) The curtain call of a supporting actor. In the threesome you and your murderer video your cock is smaller and you come first. He is cut and moans more convincingly, the lithe young pro becomes orgasmic against his hard electric frame. You are greyer and fatter than Hogan, almost Schultz-like in your breathing, asthmatic behind the betacam, directing your final scene. The Carolinas and a tripod were the death of you. Impotent tragedian, your libidinal necrosis a postmortem humiliation. Bludgeoned on the cutting-room floor, America's *Gotterdammerung*. I lay in the motel bed staring at the indigo pulse of the fire alarm. Terrified of dying in the cell of this kind of conflagration since Brian's mother Huegette perished in New York. My family is asleep around me. There will be more violence. Simultaneous diarrhea and vomiting. After hearing of your demise on a top 40 station my father parked the rental in the *Shakey's Pizza* lot. I mourned your passing with Kinch and Carter, Newkirk and Lebeau, a Coke and ptomaine. I hummed the theme song march through dessert imagining Richard Dawson refusing a kiss, cancelling that evening's taping of *The Family Feud*. Colonel Crightendon would say "I outranked him by a day" to anyone who'd listen. Even Klink would remove his monocle to salute a noble foe. This occurs before my voice changes: I could sing then, a beautiful tenor, and impersonate you flawlessly. Bob, we still share this inscrutable gaze and predatory grin, a mischievous love of perplexing Nazis, and the ability to reinforce endless tunnels with desire. Never daring to entertain even the hope of escape is a visceral response to our passionate claustrophobia.

WAVERLY HOTEL

Three rooms for the characters of religious consummation; ponytailed schoolgirl, dipsomaniacal aunt, bestfriend's mother. To Mary the rapture, attending my tendencies, wounds, and visions. Not roleplay but transubstantiation. Anointed with Cheetos and pop, cigarettes and Trojans. *Sure there is no saving a gone world with the transparent blandishments of your personal pain and the necessary details of your sex life.* But the declension of this embrace is in the *Invisible World* of the beaten woman battering your door. Tender ministrations and mercy calls, the payphone across the hall. Her lover pleading "baby baby, I'm sorry please come back baby, get the fuck in here bitch." Watching a roach bisect the ceiling I roll back across your collarbone, press lips into your neck and whisper a hill of skulls.

Christian Bök

from CRYSTALLIZATION
for Steve McCaffery

Acrylic is to zinc as lycra is
to talc. Catalytic nitro.
Triazolyl. All, tall, stall.
Zircons in tiaras allay no
tonsilitis. Acyl intranatal lacy
tactor rotor alinasal rostral
actor. Latin stannic tannin
tinctorial tyrant cyan nitriary
sty. Citation is corrosion,
not a sacral catallactics.
Itaconic. Cytolytic arylation.
Liar, lira, lair. Iconoclastic,
I cast coins on any altar tray.
Total alintatao aortitis.
Antiarin. Sacrosanct, a traitor
to an artist is a saint
in isolation. Anionic
or cationic. Octanol. Ocarinas,
tinny on a train in transit.
Yttric alcaic air sac alacrity
tantalic acral scarlatina.
Conic acron conarial contrail
canis connation coronis acariosis.
Solar, sonic, sonar. No
conciliator sits on a star. I
install a cyclotron. Stylization.

•

Rayon is to cotton as nylon is
to satin. Collossal silo.
Tritolyl. Toll, loss, toss.
Stanzas, cantos, can concoct
acrostics. Acylal aortic calcic

iris tacit icon isotron cast-iron.
Aryan iliac colitis oolitic
actinost otosis antilysis stasis.
Artistry is cranioclasis,
not a coital titillation.
Arsanilic. Cyanitic calcitration.
Alias, alas, salsa. Antisocial,
I still insist, only a notary
or an analyst can call a clitoris
an incision. Loyal alliin
institor. Niacin. Sartorial,
a corsair tailors all coats
to a collar, to an ascot,
to a lai. Anticlinal
or cataclinal. Alizarin.
Carillons, sonorant in a starlit
city. Clonic lincoln cannon clint
contraction calin lacis cytolysin.
Citric triassic cantata caritas
carrocio intact sacristan
constantia. Noon, soon, loon.
No cyanocittas trill a tirralirra.
I lasso lariats. Ionization.

●

Salty is to carcass as tasty is
to carrion. Tantric arioso.
Alanyl. Can, cant, scant.
Royal lions roar at a lictor
too snazzy to carry a zinnia.
Lactyl styrol lysis syncrisis
nasty nitrocotton action arsis.
Asian tain ionic stain astasia
strain azoic synostosis.
Translation is anacrisis,
not a scansorial transition.
Octanoic. Intrastratal
intrication. Tin, tint, stint.
Narcissistic, I occasionally
contort to solicit castration.
Astral allantois isotac.
Santalin. Nationalistic,

154 Carnival

tyranny is a class act to any
aristocracy, or so say czarinas
at carnal coronations in ritzy
salons, clinics, or casinos.
Naricorn or nasicorn. Orcinol.
Catalinas, natatory
to an octoroon. Inaction anon
actinon atactic actinaria
inartistic aconitic actinistia.
Coal, cool, cola. No intinction
anoints a croissant. I cancan
or carioca. Localization.

•

Sissy is to sassy as ninny is
to nanny. Ancillary solo.
Acrylyl. Loin, loan, lanolin.
Cilia loll in a statocyst.
Nitryl notion nictitant
contrition incarnation olitory
litany otoconia. Italy taco
siltation saltato siciliano
consistorial trinitrin tornaria.
Connotation is otiosity,
not an ataractic concinnity.
Lactic. Actinic irisation.
Ort, rot, tor. Satirical,
I crisscross across all
canonical orisons. Antsy
syssarcosis isocracy. Colicin.
Anticrotalic, anisocytosis
in any aorta can clot its
sinoatrial coronary. Allision
or collision. Carotol.
Incisors, carnassial in cats.
Carats alar talons cascaron
transact sacrist antic cataract.
Rattan tisty-tosty torc toral
tyrant tit titania tarot.
Isotactic, isostatic, isotonic.
No sin on tan is cos. I coin
canasta. Crystallization.

Christine Slater

from THE SMALL MATTER OF GETTING THERE

Dimitra showed him more paper. He just kept nodding. This was all so big. Such big paper.

"You can have a page of acknowledgements, if you like," she said. "Or a dedication... Is there anyone you'd like to dedicate it to?" Kay came down then, wearing white jeans.

Mal slid a hand across his hair. He actually sighed.

"Yeah, to Lee, I guess... To my wife."

Dimitra glanced at Kay. Kay was examining her black zippered boots. She walked him up the stairs and down the passageway. Her hands were in her pockets where there was so little room for them.

"You never told me," she said quietly, "you were married." She looked at him suddenly. Mal looked back. "Must have slipped your mind, mmmh?"

(From Mal's diary: 27th October)
I was supposed to feel guilty, I suppose, and did. I left the house as furtively as if I'd robbed it. It helped that it had begun to rain so I had an excuse to run.

Whenever I go to Kay's, I just sit there thinking how small I seem in that world. How obvious. I hate myself for assuming it matters. And I think it matters to Kay that I'm married...

"Well," Kay said. "I'm stunned."

"So am I," said Dimitra. "He's just a kid."

Kay stood at the bottom of the steps.

"It's not that. Most of us marry as kids." She paused. "You never heard this from me, but it doesn't fit with the image, know what I mean? And the little sod should have planned it better."

"Mal's getting his book published..." Lee said it proudly, but still he winced. Her parents traded blanked out glances over the plastic centre-piece.

"Well, there you go," Lee's dad said, his elbows fixed firmly on the table as if preparing for combat with his knife and fork. "Goin' to be makin' any money off it?"

Mal nodded. Her mother urged more potatoes, her face concentrated and quiet. He took the bowl from her.

"That's the problem, then, I should think. You get all the upfront money, but you gotta say your prayers somebody buys it, so's you get some more. And then there's always the other one you gotta write. It's not exactly steady, is it? Could be worse'n punchin' in every day, wouldn't you say?" He grinned; Mal missed it. "Despite the bloody glory."

"Yeah," Mal answered, slamming potatoes onto his plate. "I'd say so."

Mal recognized Kay's footsteps on the outside stairs. She always seemed in such a hurry to him — the long strides she took, her shoulders squared and purposeful. Sitting in the front office silence, Dimitra agreeably letting him in and now busy beneath him, he wondered what Kay did for fun. Then Mal heard the crisp warp of a paper bag and the rattle of key ring — there was the sound of some juggling, some struggle — and wondered if he ought to get the door and decided not to. He shouldn't even be there; he had no business opening her door.

Kay let herself in swearing. She wrenched the bag, ripping it. His shadow fell into the hall mirror. For a second she was startled. Then she smiled when she said, "Well, help me, damn it," and something funnily foreign entered and relaxed him. He liked the way she looked at him. He felt almost expected.

She steered him to a bar down the street. It was mid-afternoon and the place was close to empty. They took a table by the window, the King's Road busy and oblivious on the other side of it. She ordered a gin and tonic speculatively, eyeing the bottles from afar, as if, Mal thought, unfamiliar with hard liquor. She was still smiling when the glass came.

"So to what do I owe the honour?" she said. "Is there anything else you'd like to tell me? Besides the wife, I mean. Any convictions, perhaps, or a terminal disease?"

He laughed.

"Pissed you off, that, didn't it?"

She waved her hand mildly, dismissively, but her words had such an edge he felt almost skewered.

"I was going to say it's not my business, but I suppose it is in a small way. You might've told me earlier. You appeared to have omitted it from your life story."

He gazed into his beer.

"I forgot," he said. His face was oddly earnest; hers openly skeptical. "No, really, I was overwhelmed." He paused. "And when I remembered, I was still overwhelmed. You overwhelmed me. It didn't seem like something you'd want to hear, from what you said about the book and all."

"Is it something you're ashamed of?"

"I don't think so," he said. There was a pause so big you could bury a body in it.

"Why don't you wear a ring, then?" she asked.

"Because," he answered. "I could afford only one."

She lay listless upstairs, every young male face on TV reminding her of Mal. And, falling asleep in the swish of the evening wind, she heard his voice saying over and over that she overwhelmed him.

(From Mal's diary: 30th October)

I don't know why I did it. Why I went there in the fucking first place, why I sat with her in the pub, why I insisted on paying because I felt I owed her more than the explanation, why, because of it, I felt we were on some kind of date. And I don't know why too big a part of me enjoyed it in a seedy, shy and secretive way. On the way home, I wondered, for the first time I cared to admit, what she'd be like to sleep with.

He was sitting on the edge of an unmade bed. The shade swung in the wind.

"I'm having a few people over on Friday," she said. "It's sort of business. Sucking up to the trade, you know?"

He laughed.

"Would you come? I'm sure it's hardly your idea of a good time, but it wouldn't hurt to get used to it."

"Is this called a good career move?"

"You tell me after the party."

"Yeah, all right," he said. "If you want."

158 Carnival

"Your wife's welcome, Mal." Kay's voice was very level.

"Thanks," he said. "I'll have to ask her."

(From Mal's diary: 3rd November)

When she got in, I was shaving. She stood in the doorway, still in her jacket.

"You aimin' to go out?" she asked.

"Yeah," I said. "It's about the book."

She said oh, and turned away.

"You might have told me, you know. I could have made my own plans."

"Sorry," I said, lying. "It just came up. It won't be long. Just a drink."

I remember nudging her with the hand that held the razor. "I have to meet the right people, don't I?"

She just looked at me and said she thought I already had...

Paul Dutton

KIT-TALK

mutter to tight head stutter at stick-tip pepper past rim-pulled skin held taut: got a little. got a lot. got a metal-splash sizzle as excess is, as is a zero's eyes assessing assizes. put. put put. put. pause. put in a pause. put in a pause 'n' snap. put in a pause 'n' snap off a sizeable bit to tip a put-up past a pot-head patsy whose tight-lipped two-timing's tapered off. tapered-off top-spin whispers hisses at a brush-back pitch sent to size up what type o' sissy's up to bat. tough tit, kid, but suck it, suck it, suck it till its tender, 'n' suck it, suck it, suck it till its tip is stiff as a stick, 'n' suck it, suck it, suck it, suck it, suck. suck at it. suck at it. suck at it till it tingles. suck at it till it tingles and its spit-wet tip can't take it. shhh. shhh. she's sighin', sure as shootin' she's not shy shit no she's shirtless 'n' shameless she's shorts-down dyin' to do it 'n' here's to it. to it 'n' at it. to it 'n' at it 'n' overnight. good night. good good good good good good night. good good good good good good day. good good good good good good time. good. good good. good good good good, good 'n' gooder. gooder in the gutter. got 'er gooder in the gutter 'n' took it up top to clatter that tick on a metal bit clatter his stick on a metal bit tip took off on a pulled down pop-pulled pow paid pat paid peter paid paul paid cash-strapped fish-store short shrift for switching from fish-stick sales to hash-stick pushing to doped-up wish-merchants waiting by wash-stands in run-down walkways past push-stick talk, paid pull-down pow-wow walkway west, way hey-down, hoe-down, who got gone gained getalong ghost, gained go round goalie has got that puck, has got that puck and won't let go, has got that puck and will let you, let one, let all, let no one in, let this be it till dream-drip trickle-up pushes past top-down tail tipped sold out sin-fest lips slide slipping off flesh flaps flipped for fuller fooling round with chunk of punch-drunk monkey-mind spun down, wrung out, hard-held think unthunk. plunk.

SHY THOUGHT

There's something about always saying the same thing over and over again usually making it different all the time talking about what disappears when it's talked of, saying again what was already said differently around what won't stay still that keeps it somehow close. It's the same thing talking about always saying around something being about near what it is. Just what's usually always different about which one anyway's disappearing is still what it won't let be said about what's put differently, wanting not to stop repeating what's almost been said. Same again. Speaking of saying over and over what's always somehow almost being said, it's not just there but here again somewhere being different still. There's always something about saying things over that's usually different each time it's there in peripheral cognition. See? The same old thing. There's something always about, something always talking about, something somewhere always talking about almost saying something exactly the same way nearly every time it's said over and practically there out of the corner of your mind differently again. Again, it's not the same thing. Something else is the same thing differently another time somewhere that it's not being talked of but around again.

BARK

Last night I barked
and a dog shut up.

This morning I purred
and the cat came in.

Tomorrow I'm gonna buzz
and see what happens.

Lea Harper

WEEKEND INDIANS

Invitation to the Sweat Lodge
A real estate agent finds out
she has sold hundreds into mortgage slavery
because the natives here claim the land
does not belong to us, we belong to the land
and surely every house on the crowded block
owns its inhabitants

Before entering the womb
you leave behind your clothes and jewelry
The souls of the ancestors circle overhead
like hungry hawks
Offer them tobacco, table scraps —
they're happy

The earth is opening
the walls of the body
weeping primordial fluid
the first breath of rarefied air
thicker than a membrane

Cedar ignites its tinsel
(the pipe, a faultless conductor
once it's touched the fire stone)
and the thundergods inhale your prayer
like smoke

She prays with a handful of sage over her mouth
her lungs in cinders
prays she won't faint… or die
prays the Mayan with the long braid sees her
in the erotic glow of the pipe bowl
understands her commitment to his people
her willingness to endure this torture
But his brains are scrambled like re-fried beans
from serving 500 years of colonialism
and he regards her with mute suspicion

Panic
    Imagine dragging your tongue
    over the entire geography of Central America
    recovering every expropriated peso
    Pray with your knees straddling his hips
    if you must. Taste the salt of the earth
Unbearable heat
    Concentrate. Pray to close a deal
    so you can spend more time being spiritual —
    Severed lots, subdivisions in the company name
    Count them like sheep
Gasping
    Remember the eagle claw clasping the crystal ball
    Hold it up to the moon
    Tell your grandmother you're sorry
    you missed her funeral
    Pretend you are tanning at Club Med

The medicine man is putting on his buffalo headdress
with the ermine tails
There are no bison in Guelph
and the Sioux are starving on a uranium field
in South Dakota
but there are still painted ponies

164 Carnival

Afterwards you empty your bladder
on a bed of trillium
Acres and acres of corn rise up against you
crickets shrieking —
exploiter of green spaces
squatting on crown land
your corporate scratch pad
mere bum wipe here

Take heart
Tonight you were evicted from the world
like a spirit
You were jaguar woman, fawn child
carrying strong snake medicine
Never mind the morning
when you'll threaten the dry cleaners
with the roll-on stain at the armpit
of your silk blouse
your high heels gouging the lawn
like furious tent pegs
your nylons snagging on those blasted bushes again

The voice on the answering machine will be anyone
but God and the Mayan
If you're lucky you'll hear 'Metal Ecstasy'
pound the pavement all the way down Queen Street
Everyone there has black hair and a handbag
from Guatemala

Buy some time, a little wine
maybe squeeze a vision from the fitful night
some credibility to bring to the circle
and pass around like a postcard
come next weekend

BIRTH

"I am waiting for the rebirth of wonder"
— Lawrence Ferlinghetti

So this is the miracle you have waited for
like an armful of winter flowers
the dream's blue flame touching down

It seems impossible
just yesterday
you moved like a bloated inchworm
through the smouldering summer
your belly of yeast rising
on a nine month timer
touchy as a swollen gland
a cellar toad
its green appetite
souring like apples

And the knowing sisters nod
assure and console
'It is all natural'
the skin drawn tight as a cowhide drum
with its patchy pigmentation
blackened nipples and wobbly brown line
like a surgical sign
from breastbone to groin

And when the time comes
natural too, the pain
in sickening waves, with tidal force
lobster vice and scorpion pincers
tusk of wild boar
the breaking through, the tearing open
a stone boat bearing down the perilous chasm
a quaking flood of blood

And with her sucking —
a sharp, needling determination
the aftershock of contractions
the sleepless night, the ravenous sterling cry
a blind starling's tuneless song
and your body sagging, its loose flesh
like an empty paper bag

Then the eyes open like cathedral windows
on a grey world
gaze up at your face
in love and trust and wonder
her hands tiny swans or breezy clouds waving
her pink bud mouth opening into smiles
Are you worthy of the gift?
Are you ready to live
and die for her?
Hold her precious above all things?
Her signature is written in your blood
an indelible contract
Every cell sings yes
Nothing will ever be this perfect
and clear again

Sky Gilbert

WHY THIS POEM IS NOT ANYTHING LIKE BROCCOLI

This poem is not good for you
And it's not green
It's not boring (at least I hope not)
And your mother probably wouldn't tell you to read this
poem the way she would tell you to eat broccoli
In fact she might even tell you to stay away from it
What I'm really writing here is an unhealthy poem
It's not good for you
It could be bad for you
But what isn't?
I mean I just heard yesterday that all the drinking water that we get from
the Niagara River has Dioxin in it and it's the Americans who are
putting the Dioxin in the water, right, and like you know how hard
it is to get those Americans to stop doing anything if they don't
want to and why should they want to?
So don't worry about reading this poem that is bad for you because it's
not half as bad for you as drinking water
And you probably won't read this poem again whereas with water well,
I'll bet you'll have two glasses just like that
But to get down to basics, that is what makes this poem not necessarily
good for you
Well, just so as not to keep you in suspense it's because I'm going to
romanticize all out of proportion having sex with this guy who I
hardly know
Now I know human beings need love and nourishment and encourage-
ment and you should only have sex with people you know and that
are very clean looking and have good teeth and who like, work out
where you work out

But this time I couldn't manage all that
He's about 23 and he wants to be an actor
Except that right now he works for a credit company
He wears the kind of coats you wear when you haven't got much money
   (Tower's coats) and from far away he looks like the most beautiful
   boy in the world
No really
Up close he looks a little sick
And I got drunk for three Friday nights in a row and picked him up at
   the Barn and we have a great time in bed
And having sex with him is nothing like eating broccoli
And I know I'm not supposed to be promiscuous anymore but I followed
   most of the rules (there are so many now) and he cut his hand I
   have to tell you this part he cut his hand and I put ointment on it
   and he must have fallen asleep three or four times and just rested his
   handsome, sickly, young, tortured head on my chest the same
   number of times while sleeping
It was like being in heaven when he did that
So now I'm going to analyze what happened in four different modes in an
   attempt to make this into a healthy poem

psychoanalytic:
I have no self-respect and therefore don't think I deserve a doctor or a
   lawyer or a computer programmer and thus in order to degrade
   myself I pick up boys in Tower's jackets of different descriptions in
   order to feel bad about myself as I'm not comfortable with feeling
   good
Also there seems to be an element of self-destruction in me as I say I
   followed most of the rules about sexual safety but not all I should
   learn to be my one best friend

romantic:
I just met the most beautiful boy in the world and he's not particularly
   well-educated but I'm sure he's perceptive and so sweet and loving
   and he needs love and needs me and I could live with him and teach
   him and make him into a human being just like me only who would
   take care of me
I hope he calls

artistic:
I sure have been getting bored lately and I haven't written a poem for a
     month and I have to do this reading for the Gays and Lesbians in
     Health Care and I hate doing just old poems so if I fuck somebody
     beautiful then I have something to write a poem about and it's
     usually a good poem if the guy is really beautiful and wrong for me in
     every way the poem is usually great
So that's why I did it

sexual:
I was horny and he was a great lay
Like really great

So, those are all the modes of analysis and if you put them all together
     you probably have a vague idea of why I do these things but I did
     have one revelation in the middle of it all which I think explains
     why this poem is not like broccoli and it's going to get graphic now
     so hold onto your plates — we were doing it with a condom but of
     course I had to keep looking at the condom to make sure it didn't
     break but I had this revelation just before coming which was — sex
     shouldn't be quite so wrapped up with death should it? I mean yes
     coming is sort of like dying and dying is in fact a metaphor for
     orgasm in some literature but should I actually be worrying about
     dying all the time now when I'm having sex?
I don't think so
I'm going to do a mixture of all the modes of analysis and finish this
     poem
I had this experience with this boy in the coat from Tower's that was too
     big for him and probably belonged to his brother because I don't
     deserve a computer programmer and I sure have been getting bored
     lately and I was horny and he was a great lay and I hope he calls
That's my unhealthy poem
Eat some broccoli
Now
But don't you have water with it

Breakfast in Key West

Ahh, the New York Times
Lots of rye toast
Four white boys, bronze tits and rumpled tummies bared to the sun
Their favourite faghag laughing at their jokes
The strawberries are fresh and everybody feels like a pornstar
When suddenly, a cloud
A very large black man and his lover (who is slender but exquisitely
     ugly) step out upon the deck
     conversation stops
All look down and read intently
As if in prayer
And that's what it's like really if somebody is really ugly
     or different or something
It spoils our perfect whiteboy breakfast
And we look away and pray
Never to be that ugly or that different
Like the ads for starving children
And that's why I like having a boyfriend that's not perfectly beautiful I
     mean I think he is but to other people I think he might appear to be
     just a normal guy but that's okay
because he has special secret places and beauties that only I know about
     and he stands in front of the mirror for hours (thank god for boys
     who do that) and arranges his hair well maybe not hours but I know
     he'll never be perfect and neither will I and if we get old together
     and go to Key West we'll stop lunches too, we will be exquisitely
     ugly and different and loud and déclassé
So just remember
When you're having breakfast
Under the sun
And the imperfect ugly different beggar who's not like you
walks by
It's really an angel passing over
Yes, it's time to pray.

Lynn Crosbie

PEARL

Ande precious perles unto his pay.
            Amen, Amen.

Valentine, bishop of Interamna waited for execution in his cell
this February. Heart-shaped florets arrayed on his desk —
the Lupercalian festival. Winter,

cold spider-nevi, misting his window-glass.

He had shaved his head into a smooth pearl, some months earlier.
The last time I saw him I looked away. His delicate scalp,
the low, menacing whistle, afraid of him.

>   I thought he was powerful because of his contempt,
>   his anger. His silk-yellow hair, sheared; I had
>   wanted to touch this

sleek daffodil, once. His eyes are seawater; their calm blue surface belies
what is beneath — fire-coral, stingrays.

>   I saw water on his kitchen floor and called out anxiously
>   to him, I thought you were dead, I thought you were dead.

Dressed in red on Valentine's Day — crimson ribbons, lips and bows,
        I answer the telephone:
John is dead, I'm sorry, he killed himself last night.

I walk to his apartment and climb the stairs. The hallway is
        sweet smelling,
cloying; his door is in flames, prohibiting entrance.

172 Carnival

I will see him again, and again.

At the morgue — his mottled face arched against the metal frame,
     only his forehead is recognizable.
A pale expanse, it looks like bliss, as smooth as stone.

And in dreams — he kisses me with awkward passion; he is telling me,
     what he has found.
He was so uneasy, with gestures, with love: *The thought of having
     close friends frightens me.*
I never touched him, I gave him roses instead.

The way that roses die, their scarlet flush betrayed by the careless sepal.
The thorns provide little protection, the thorns

like the bowl of water, offer a half-life: they are dead already.

His rooms already vacant, empty datebooks, a small framed photograph
     of Yukio Mishima:
Beauty, beautiful things… those are now my most deadly enemies.

   His pink knit blanket strewn on the floor, the depressions
   in the pillows. A ring of tiny keys, an empty vial:
   I have taken 45-50 Ativan, I did not plan to write this letter.

I think of the plastic shroud intoxicating him, his breath becoming
     narcotic; there is nothing here.
In the absence, of regret and menace, I gather his suicide detritus,
and seal it in a paper bag,

where I have entombed his last answering-machine message: *I haven't
     talked to you in a while,*
call me,

He asked that his notebooks be burned — the fire that has now erased him,
tissue, marrow, bone, unfolding, a whisper, *I did not plan to*

I find that he has forgiven me, too late. An outline in his notes
    (there were folders, flat, unrequited desires)
plots a story, where I appear, with an electric guitar and
a strange fit, of prescience:

> * *The time she came to my apartment and saw water on the floor
> & thought I was dead.*

The memories and affections he buried, frail green shoots in fallow
    underground. Lost
in ineffable misery; *he turns once more*, to what is left.
    Heartbreak —
two tattered slippers, a window with a view of asphalt, metal stairs.

His lustrous head in its oyster shell — he rattles as he surrenders
    an obscure ghost.
I have never been religious, his spirit enters strangers, machines,
    a photograph.

Taken as I watched, a summer morning, I thought, for the first time,
    he was beautiful.
Serene and knowing — grey clouds have descended on this still frame,

clouds portending

I will call you, many times — sometimes I will berate you, my *partner
in crime*, and sometimes, I will ask you,
to take me with you.

David Donnell

WHAT'S SO EASY ABOUT 17?

I don't know what it is about youth
except for an honest desire to concentrate on textbooks
of infinitesimal calculus,
&   & at the same time a great love
of carelessness,
                    a wanton energy,
throwing their shoulders around as if ecstasy is movement
or motion is ecstasy,
                    a wantonness, a carelessness so
beautiful that like a warm summer breeze you lift
your hand up to your red hair
in amazement & open your mouth to taste the fine grains
of copper magnesium cobalt in the summer air.

In Tobacco Heaven my friends are killed
on freeways. Smoking dope perhaps, or a fifth of cheap liquor.
They are about 17, tall & slim,
                         usually wearing t-s
or sloppy shirts;
                    except for Carson who was short & plump
the class clown, with a flat-top haircut,
who went through a guard rail in a red Mazda
& fell 135 feet.

A boy with the body of a
perfect high school basketball star
long torso no waist & the smile of a sardonic angel
my name is John,
                    call me Johnny Slow Hand,
driving
with a large unadulterated jumbo of Coke
Joan Crawford's favourite drink.
It makes me nauseous, she once said,
between his long legs,
                    radio blaring Elton John
that song about how the blues will always come back
with brass in the background
                              a lift from LA Express
caught the tail of a grey Plymouth
making a lazy turn no tail-lights onto a country side road
& was then clipped by 3 cars & a truck
                              & flipped
on the boulevard.

          Saturday night
the cars have to be cut open with an acetylene torch
to lift their once perfect Adidas-shod bodies
out of the wrecked car the way you would lift an egg out
of a crushed bird's nest.
                    Mostly boys,
the girl was an exception, & under the age of 29.
Boys have the big A-stat. A for accident
& A for a sort of hyper-tense anxiety
backed up by a tumultuous review of hormones.
Boys are expressive, sure, okay,
& also aggressive drivers.

     Jerzy Kosinski
snuffed out with a plastic bag.
Surely you weren't trying to do anything like that?
When you're 17 1/2 the world is a huge 6/5ths.
6/5ths of a gigantic moon.
                    Cut throat of the sun.

Slashed wrists of the moon.
                              You just put your foot
on the gas a little too hard with one arm out the window
& leaned back like a lazy greyhound on the comfortable
seat.
        Cut throat of the sun.
                              Slashed wrists of
the moon.
              6/5ths of the dark night.

            Tobacco Heaven lays out
the coloured highway signs from Thunder Bay to New Mexico.
Life is almost always beautiful
                              or at worst a bit of a down.
The upside on the girl is that she wasn't decapitated,
unlike the Hispanic kid who was
driving with his feet just to prove he could do it.
Can you do it Jaime can you do it Jaime can you do it Jaime?
Si,
    it is easy, I can/
                    do it.
And if you lose control
then the night road is wrong because
it has imperfect highway seals under the asphalt
some designs don't breathe the way a highway
should breathe. Some axles lock, & some don't.
Driving with your knees only is strictly forbidden
while eating pizza
                    turning over a tape cassette
or changing your shirt.
The Buzzcocks should never have broken up
when they were so so good. Some curves
in the highway are actually a dark blue parallel.
Some high schools have good basketball teams
with cheerleaders & some don't. All highway signs
should be *illuminated*. Some windshields
break more easily than others.

bill bissett

I WAS DRIVING IN 2 HUNDRID MILE HOUS
IN TH KARIBU NORTHERN BC

n saw big sign on th left sd
ANIMAL HOSPITAL, thot 2
myself well thers nothing reelee
wrong with me now but if i take
anee turn 4 th wors i cud go in
2 see doktor racoon or nurs squirrel
its reassuring 2 know thers help
sew close by   well wud yu go
in2 a building sd PEOPUL HOSPITAL
iuv bin with peopul

WHO HAS SEEN TH DEFISIT

our leedrs wudint tell us a storee a
ficksyun o
no disgraceful potash sircumstances madam
cumstances apoth e oasis apothee cary went
wild evree time don was in 2 him psychikalee
or as th streem neembsee pretend various x
pektaysyuns arriving
th purpos uv th rhetorik
uv th ruling klasses is 2 make us pesants feel bad
evn guiltee not ourselvs
n our leedrs 2 knee jerk
cut n slash whn th i m f sz sew imf imf we watch
totalee objekting whil our leedrs steel from th poor
n give 2 th rich
robert mcnamarra sd he was sorree
abt th war in vietnam   that it had bin a mistake OOPS
th ovr 3 millyun killd aftr that war he was appointid
ths was in reel life wun uv th heds uv th i m f

in 20 or sew yeers will mcnamarra write anothr book
saying hes sorree abt busting th yuunyuns creating
a world wide undrklass as a result uv free trade global
restrukshuring deels n insistens on veree low key
soshul programs strip govrnment th pesants owe big
time leedrs veree rich cant owe as a result uv
poliseez uv i m f mcnamarra was 4 a time hed uv

th peopul returnd 2 themselvs she
carreed ths othr his hed wrappd in towels filld with
ths leedrs blood th carriage going fastr n fastr back
2 th pastoral medow n appul tree places deep in
larkspur n raven song
th hot gold glaysing eye uv
th green n bountiful hill side his hed singing ovr th
rich n deep equalitee song blood all wayze running
on th post whn wud it dry his sew beautee hed
was resting nevr resting stuk on beeming

as we leev now th gods uv manee xcuses n burn our
skin on th freshlee erodid   sun

LET TH WATR SIT 4 A DAY   N TH
CHLOREEN EVAPORATES

we livd on top uv a glass hill   wher
        evreething was alredee with us   no
seering need 2 serch th crevices uv th inside
        uv th startchd stretchd purpul caverna
        dank full uv echoez clattring suddnlee on th
bronze stone   luminous in its chillee unfold
        ing 4 watr suppliez projekts possibiliteez
or love without wch aftr all   tho th life uv
th imaginaysyun nevr faltrs   it can go on un
heedid by prescripsyun n evenshulee evree thing
        fails   yet inbtween thos polariteez xtreems
thers a lot uv life 2 life   we tuk a look outside
        it was incrediblee dens th fog   th swirling un
known   entiteez   obviouslee shut off th volume
        on th wide band announsr n maroond ourselvs
        gentlee on th rockee ledg n waitid
        found among th flowrs wer items uv all our
                dreems n sighing   its veree beautiful by th
see side   drinking xcellent koffee by th
        fresh ocean spray   uv kours its sumtimes
        rockee   changing schedules n rhythms eye
        dont assess it   seulment support it whatevr
        its all 4 lerning   acceptans n watching th
        big waves change   "... hi its veree lovlee
        by th seeside   at last finding pees n content
ment   in xcellent companee n th waves ar sew
tall n th koffee sew fabulous   we feel we cud bathe
        in th sunshine   well past infinitee..." i got my
sunnee opia thru wun uv my travls thru southern
centralia   now ium laffing by th see shore spinning
        storeez uv motivaysyun n othr peopul with a
        close frend   theereez uv relaysyunships its
        wundrful by th seeside sew warm n magikul
        n we laffd at th daring lines uv th lyrik from
        th old song *green slimee wishes* ".. hes an
        xploding gazoleen tank a shrapnel cutee..."

        now at last we cud laff at almost aneething

Biographies

1995

WENDY AGNEW is a writer, director, actor, performance artist, illustrator and teacher. *The Lillian Lectures*, a series of lessons on the mysteries of life, are available as individually illustrated, hand-bound books. She is a co-founder and co-director of Pow Pow Unbound, the company that astounded Toronto's theatre community with *Stage* and *Field*.

ANDRÉ ALEXIS was born in Trinidad and came to Canada at age three. At the Scream he read from *Despair And other Stories Of Ottawa* (Coach House Press), his first collection of fiction. A novel is forthcoming. His plays, such as *Hunger, Home* and *Faith*, have played in Toronto and Vancouver.

JOHN BARLOW turned the Scream stage into his living room and recruited us for the Oversion Party. In his words he: "loves and prefers psychic poetry as an alternative universe. Not unreal, though it may appear to be unreal. Loves the lost landscape of the unwritable memories of silent unprovable incarnations as they manifest on the surface of the water looking up from under and hearing it in the heavens as they collapse in the narrowing that is time." His collection of poetry, *Safe Telepathy* (1996), is published by Exile Editions.

JAYMZ BEE is best known as the front man, singer and songwriter for the enigmatic bands Look People and Jaymz Bee and His Royal Jelly Orchestra (their self-titled album was reissued by BMG). During his performance at Scream he was accompanied by Great Bob Scott who turned the stage into a found percussion instruments. He is a recording artist, record producer, video director and almost anything that requires an imagination.

NICOLE BROSSARD is a two-time Governor General award winner [*Mecanique jonglease* (Daydream Mechanics), 1975, and *Double Impression*, 1984]. She has written 19 collections of poetry, eight novels, a play and several pieces for radio. Born and presently living in Montreal, she has founded two feminist journals and co-edited an *Anthology of Quebec Women Poets*. Nicole also co-directed the documentary Some American Feminists. Her most recent novel is *Baroque at Dawn* (Coach House Press). *Matter Harmonious Still Maneuvering* was her closing poem at the Scream.

CLAIRE HARRIS was the winner of the 1984 Commonwealth Prize for poetry (*Fables From The Women's Quarters*) and was nominated for the 1993 Governor General's Award (*Drawing Down A Daughter*). Born in Trinidad and widely travelled, she now resides in Calgary, where she teaches. At the Scream, Claire read *Grammar of The Heart* from *The Conception Of Winter*. Her most recent collection is *Dipped in Shadow* (Goose Lane Editions).

DANNABANG KUWABONG taught the audience a folksong that his grandmother had taught him: Ye bang ka a kamaana deme / Yele ba kamaana yele (Know the maize owners / Talk about their maize). He is a native of Ghana and currently lives in Hamilton, Ontario. He has a book of poetry *Visions of Venom* (1995, Woeli Publishing Services, Accra) and *Naa Konga: A Collection of Dagaaba Folktales* was published in 1992. Dannabang is completing a Ph.D. on the language of Caribbean poetry in English. He is currently seeking a publisher for a poetry manuscript, *Echoes of Reeds — X-Ray of a Hollow Skull*.

ELISE LEVINE is a co-winner of the 1994 PRISM International Short Fiction Award and has twice been nominated for the Journey Prize. Elise read from her first short fiction collection, *Driving Men Mad* (1995, Porcupine's Quill) at the Scream. Cave diving is among her many interests and inspirations.

EILEEN O'TOOLE sings, writes and acts. She played a mean ukulele at Scream In High Park. Her series of monologues, *Lester's Girlfriend*, are published as a collection by Gutter Press and Shard Press. She sings with the glamorous Ukulele Sisters and leads a Celtic pub band. Toronto's independent theatre community has honoured Eileen with a Harold Award.

MATTHEW REMSKI is the founder and original artistic director of Scream In High Park. His first book, *Organon Vocis Organalis (Book II of Aerial Sonography)* published and designed by Stan Bevington, won the 1994 bp nichol chapbook award. His work can also be found in the

Insomniac Press anthology *Mad Angels and Amphetamines*. In 1994, he documented an international installation symposium near Prague. Matthew currently lives in Vermont. At the Scream he read from *dying for veronica*, a novel to be published by Insomniac Press in 1997.

STUART ROSS is a poet, fiction writer, sound poet, performer, editor, publisher, and small press activist. He has published 12 books of poetry and 10 works of fiction, *The Inspiration Cha-Cha* (1996, ECW), a poetry collection, and *The Mud Game* (Mercury Press), fiction in collaboration with Gary Barwin. In 1997, Mercury Press will also release *Henry Kafka*, a collection of short fiction. Stuart has collaborated with Gary on two sound poetry recordings, *These Are The Clams That I'm Breathing* and *Preacher Explodes During Sermon*.

PATRICIA SEAMAN is originally from Alberta and now lives in Toronto. She is the author of *The Black Diamond Ring* (1995, Mercury Press), *Never Forget You Look Great* (Parts 1 & 2), *Amphibian Hearts* and a novella, *Hotel Destiné*. In addition to her writing, she works with collage. She has recently completed the novel *Super Nevada*, from which we have taken an excerpt.

GERRY SHIKATANI was born in Toronto and is currently living in Montreal. He is a poet, prose writer, text-sound artist and film maker. Gerry has published nine collections of poetry including *1988 (Selected Poems 1973 -)*. Mercury Press, Underwhich Editions, and Wolsak and Wynn have collaborated to publish *Aqueduct: poems and prose from Europe 1979-87*. Mercury will also publish *Lake and Other Stories*. Gerry co-edited *Paper Doors: an anthology of Japanese-Canadian poetry*. His sound work is often influenced by the Japanese language. A sound collage, dedicated to his mother, was enthusiastically received at the Scream.

LISE WEIL is a writer and translator living in Montreal.

1994

RAFAEL BARETTO-RIVERA is one of Canada's most exciting sound poets and was the catalyst for the formation of the Four Horsemen, the renowned performance group. Born in San Juan, Puerto Rico, he is an accomplished poet, performer and translator. He has released the recording *Scrabble Babble*, the books *Nimrod's Tongue*, *Voices Noises* and most recently the chapbook *Memoranda From The Milky Way: Alex de Cosson's Sky Harp*. He read from *Shredded What: A Whitman Serial* at Scream.

NANCY BULLIS has been reading and writing in and around Toronto since the early days of the Poetry Sweatshop. Her poems and fiction have appeared in magazines such as *Toronto Life* and *Writ*. She has been an editor and a covergirl model (for *Ontario Out of Doors...* though the credits only mentioned the fish she was holding). She is a lawyer, but is not currently practicing.

LISE DOWNE in her lifetime has manufactured over 50,000 books — as a bookbinder. Primarily a visual artist, she began focussing on her poetry and produced *A Velvet Increase In Curiosity*, (ECW Press) her first collection, in 1994.

NANCY DEMBOWSKI sold funeral plots, worked for Ringling Brothers and Barnum & Bailey Circus and recruited for the National Organization for Women, before moving to Toronto from her native Washington D.C. She now attends the University of Toronto and raises her two children. Her poetry has appeared in anthologies, on CDs and on MuchMusic. Nancy's Scream performance, many have asked: 'Why haven't I heard of her before?'

CLIFTON JOSEPH has long been active on the Toronto poetry scene, and was the artistic director of the World Dub Poetry Festival. Born in Antigua, he tempers streetwise imagery with a jazz sensibility. His record *Oral Trans/missions* was selected CKLN's 1988 album of the year.

BILL KENNEDY is a poet and was co-editor of *sinovertan magazine*. He is also the keyboard player for the musical collective his uneven rhythm. He lives in Toronto and works as a freelancer. He opened 1994's Scream with *Apostrophe*, an evolving commentary on pop-culture.

KAREN MAC CORMACK is a poet and freelance editor who has worked as a gallery curator. She is the author of five books of poetry: *Nothing By Mouth, Straw Cupid, Quilldriver, Quirks and Quillets*, and most recently, *Marine Snow* (ECW).

MAC MCARTHUR lives in a country schoolhouse with two Newfoundlands. His poetry has been published in *ARC, Fiddlehead* and in the *James White Review*, the premiere U.S. gay literary magazine. His latest manuscript is *Hymn to Delicate Men: A Chronology*. He volunteers for FREE THE CHILDREN to stop exploited child labour.

STEVE MCCAFFERY is a poet, performer and internationally respected critic. He has travelled worldwide as a member of the sound poetry ensemble the Four Horsemen and is a founding member of the L=A=N=G=U=A=G=E poetry movement. *Theory of Sediment* was shortlisted for the 1993 Governor General's award for poetry. Other works include *Panopticon, The Black Debt*, and recently, *The Cheat of Words* (ECW Press).

Biographies 185

SONJA MILLS is a poet, playwright, performer and stand-up comic. Her first play, *Dyke City*, was produced as part of Queer Culture at Buddies In Bad Times, and spawned a remounting and a sequel. More of her work can be found in the Insomniac anthology *Desire High Heels Red Wine*.

SUSAN MUSGRAVE has published 19 books of poetry, fiction, children's literature and essays and has been short-listed for the Governor General's award four times. Her latest books include *Forcing The Narcissus*, a collection of poetry, and *Musgrave Landing*, essays. We will never forget the scramble to rearrange the programme when, 15 minutes before Susan was to read, an enthusiastic volunteer took the car with her books in the back seat.

M. NOURBESE PHILIP is a poet, writer and lawyer who lives in Toronto. She has published four books of poetry: *Thorns, Salmon Courage, She Tries Her Tongue; Her Silence Softly Breaks* (for which she received the prestigious Casa de las Americas prize) and *Looking For Livingstone: An Odyssey of Silence*. She has also written a children's novel, *Harriet's Daughter*. Recent non fiction work includes *Showing Grit: Showboating North of the 44th Parallel*. On stage at the Scream she said, "Let us try to keep this country what it has always been which is a country that has always welcomed people and always treats all her other peoples, based on that first act of hospitality, with a loving heart."

TRICIA POSTLE is a Toronto poet, vocalist, and hurdy-gurdy player whose work centres around food, sex and religion. She performs medieval music at various venues in and out of the city. *Today I Am A Man* was a huge hit at the Scream. More of her work can be found in the Insomniac anthology *Beds And Shotguns*.

AL PURDY has published over 30 volumes of poetry, most recently *The Woman on the Shore* and *Naked with Summer in Your Mouth*. He won his second Governor General's award in 1986 for his *Collected Poems* (the first was in 1965). He has written a novel *A Splinter in the Heart* and published his memoirs, *Reaching for the Beaufort Sea*. A new selected poems will be released in 1996 by Harbour Publishing. Al was introduced with a quote from a Milton Acorn poem... and the jungle trail cleared.

NINO RICCI's first novel *Lives of the Saints* won the Governor General's Award, the Smithbooks/Books in Canada First Novel Award and many other honours in Canada, the U.S. and Britain. *In a Glass House*, the second book in a trilogy, is published by McClelland & Stewart.

STAN ROGAL is a poet, fiction writer, playwright, actor, director, former bowling alley manager and standardized patient. He is the author of

186 Carnival

two books of poetry, *Sweet Betsy from Pike* and *The Imaginary Museum*, and a short fiction collection, *What Passes For Love*. His plays have been produced in Toronto and Vancouver and he is a founding member of the nationally recognized theatre company Bald Ego. He also runs the weekly Idler Pub Reading Series in Toronto.

LEON ROOKE has published numerous short story collections and novels, winning the Governor General's Award in 1983 for *Shakespeare's Dog*. Born in rural North Carolina, he now lives in Eden Mills, Ontario. Porcupine's Quill has published *Muffins*, a book/45-rpm record package featuring a live reading of the story. Leon had the dogs in the audience howling to his Scream appearance. He howled back.

R.M. VAUGHAN is a New Brunswick-born author, playwright and artist. His works have appeared in periodicals and anthologies throughout Canada, the U.S. and the U.K. He has had twelve plays produced and was writer in residence at Buddies In Bad Times Theatre during the 1994-1995 season. His first collection of poetry, *A Selection of Dazzling Scarves*, will be published by ECW.

DEATH WAITS is the author of two books of poetry, *My Tongue, My Teeth, Your Voice* and *62 Rock Videos for Songs That Will Never Exist*, both published by Exile Editions. His work has also been featured in the Insomniac anthology *Beds and Shotguns*. As artistic director of the Candid Stammer theatre company, Death has conceived and directed plays such as *How An Intellectual Can Aspire to Savagery*, *But Love is Too Simple to Save Us* and the dance-oriented *I Cut, You Bleed*.

1993

BILL BISSET is a poet, painter, and wonderfully impossible speller. Among his many books are *Inkorrekt Thots*, *Th last photo of th human soul* and *th influenza uv logik*, all published by Talonbooks. He has also produced several poetry/music recordings. bill closed the 1993 Scream In High Park with a sound poem that involved the entire audience.

CHRISTIAN BÖK is a poet and candidate for a Ph.D. in pataphysics. *Chrystallography*, his first book of poetry, was nominated for the Gerald Lampert Award in 1994. *Chrystalization* is an operatic sound poem that arranges a limited set of letters in a musical structure and attempts to enumerate every anagram in the title. Christian read all 12 verses of the poem at Scream In High Park without missing a syllable.

ROO BORSON is originally from California and now lives in Toronto. At the Scream, she read from her 1994 Governor General's Award nominated *Night Walk*. Among her many books are *Intent, or the Weight of the World* (1989) and *Water Memory* (1996).

LYNN CROSBIE is the author of three collections of poetry, *Miss Pamela's Mercy*, *VillainElle* and *Pearl*. She is also the editor of *The Girl Wants To*. She teaches at the Ontario College of Art in Toronto and showed the best fashion sense of anyone who has read at Scream In High Park. "Dressed in a white pageant-gown. Head slightly shaved (assymmetrically), red synthetic hairpiece, penis-man earings."

CHRISTOPHER DEWDNEY took a few moments at the Scream to tell us the names of the trees. He pointed out the park's own living fossil located on the other side of *the hill*. He then determined how the stage mic's worked by endeavouring to dismantle one. Chris has been nominated for the Governor General's Award for poetry twice for *Predators of the Adoration* and *Radiant Inventory* and once for non-fiction *The Immaculate Perception*. The selections in *Carnival* are taken from *Alter Sublime and Demon Pond*, although *The Fossil Forest of Axel Heiberg* appears here in a new version.

DAVID DONNELL won the Governor General's Award for poetry for *Settlements*. Among his many other books are *China Blues*, for which he was a co-winner of the City of Toronto Book Award, and most recently, *Dancing In The Dark* a collection of poetry and short stories. David embraced the spirit of the Scream walking on stage with an oak leaf in his hand and wondering what type of oak trees we were surrounded by.

PAUL DUTTON is the author five books of poetry including *Aurealities*. He was a member of the Four Horsemen and is an internationally renowned sound artist. He has performed at festivals which range in focus from poetry to new music. Currently, Paul is working with the free music ensemble CCMC. His performance at the Scream of *Hiding*, a work that involves chant and sound deflection to create the effect of multiple voices, was unforgettable.

SKY GILBERT is a playwright, poet, filmmaker, actor and drag queen extraordinaire. He is the co-founder and artistic director of Toronto's Buddies In Bad Times Theatre. He won Dora Awards for best new play in 1990 (*The Whore's Revenge*) and for best production in 1991 (*Suzie Goo: Private Secretary*). He has directed at the Shaw Festival and in 1985 received the Pauline McGibbon Award, presented to promising young directors. His poetry has been anthologized in *Plush* and Insomniac's *Desire High Heels Red Wine*.

BARBARA GOWDY's the author of the acclaimed novels *Through The*

Green Valley, Falling Angels, and the Governor General's award nominated, *Mister Sandman*; as well as her short fiction collection *We So Seldom Look on Love.* She lives in Toronto where she has been a teacher and broadcaster.

STEVEN HEIGHTON is the author of three books of poetry, most recently the Governor General's Award nominated, *The Ecstasy of Skeptics,* and two collections of short fiction. He is a former editor of *Quarry magazine.* Steve currently lives in Kingston where he writes and occasionally plays guitar. At the Scream he gave the first reading of his poem for Tom Marshall, *Eating The Worm.*

LEA HARPER is a recording artist and with the duo Syren received a Juno nomination. Of her experience at the Scream she says, "It was particularly exhilarating. Its natural setting, exotic lighting, invisible mic's and fabulous backdrop a curious combination of Spanish moss, Isadora's scarf and the seaweed of Ophelia's hair seemed appropriately poetic."

MICHAEL HOLMES is a poet, essayist and editor, currently completing a Ph.D. in English Literature at York University. His books of poetry include *got no flag at all* and *james i wanted to ask you.* He is the editor of *The Last Word: an insomniac anthology of contemporary Canadian literature.* At the Scream, michael read from *Satellite Dishes from the Future Bakery.* *21 Hotels* is a work in progress.

ADEENA KARASICK is dedicated to the creation and performance of language based writing. She has published two books of poetry, *MeMewars* and *The Empress has No Closure.* She is a Ph.D. candidate at Concordia University in Montreal.

PETER MCPHEE has been artistic director of Scream In High Park since 1994. *The Sound of Filling Hollow,* is a collection of his poetry on CD performed in collaboration with the musical collective his uneven rhythm and recorded live at the Music Gallery in Toronto. The 1993 Scream In High Park was his uneven rhythm's first performance.

CHRISTINE SLATER read from her first short fiction collection, *Stalking The Gilded Boneyard,* at the Scream. She has written two novels since then: *The Small Matter Of Getting There* and *Certain Dead Soldiers.*

YVES TROENDLE presented a three voice reading of *Dead Giveaway* to open the 1993 Scream In High Park. He was joined on stage by Beth and Joy Learn to perform the poem which consists of responses the artist Robert Rauschenberg had given to various interviewers, edited to form imperative statements, and written over a list of materials Rauschenberg used in his work. Among Yves' many books are *The Swallow's Testicle* and *Nothing Personal* both published by Nietzsche's Brolly.

Acknowledgements

All works printed with permission of the authors.

Matter Harmonious Still Maneuvering by Nicole Brossard first appeared in *The Massachusetts' Review*. **Mezquita** and **Who Notes: A Particular Pronoun, A Responsibility** by Gerry Shikatani reprinted from *Aqueduct* (1996, The Mercury Press, Underwhich Editions, and Wolsak and Wynn Publishers Ltd.) with permission from the author and the publishers. **Jane In Summer** and **Kay In Summer** by Claire Harris reprinted from *The Conception of Winter* (1995, Goose Lane Editions) with permission from the author and the publisher. **The Guns Of Kigali Are Silent** by Dannabang Kuwabong originally appeared in *Peace and Hope*. **dying for veronica # 72** by Matthew Remski previously appeared in *Oversion*. **Florist** and **Sam's** by Eileen O'Toole reprinted from *Lester's Girlfriend* (1993, Gutter Press and Shard Press) with permission from the author and the publisher. **Clint East Woody Allen Alda** from the album *Jaymz Bee & His Royal Jelly Orchestra* printed with permission of the author and Happy Fingers Music. Elise Levine's stories have previously appeared in different forms: **Untitled, artist's collection** in *subTERRAIN*, **True Romance** in *Blood & Aphorisms*, and **This Is It** in *Prairie Schooner*. Parts of **Shredded What: a Whitman Serial** by Rafael Barreto-Rivera appeared in *Rampike*. **Discourse On The Logic Of Language** by M. Nourbese Philip reprinted from *She Tries Her Tongue her silence softly breaks* (1989, Ragweed Press) with permission of the author. **Some Miles Asunder** by Karen Mac Cormack originally appeared in *Rampike*. **My Grandfather's Country** (in a different form) and **At The Quinte Hotel** by Al Purdy reprinted from *Being Alive* (1978, McClelland & Stewart) with permission of the author. **Novel 39** and the excerpt from **Teachable Texts** reprinted from *The Cheat of Words* (1996) with permission of the author

190 Carnival

and ECW Press. **Sweethearts** by Leon Rooke reprinted from *Who Do You Love* (1992, McClelland & Stewart) with permission of the author. **Today I'm Going To Be A Man** by Tricia Postle reprinted from *Beds and Shotguns* (1994, Insomniac Press) with permission of the author and publisher. **Dead Giveaway (re: Robert Rauschenberg)** by Yves Troendle reprinted from *Nothing Personal* (1995, Nietzsche's Brolly) with permission from the author and the publisher. **The Clouds** and **The Fossil Forest of Axel Heiberg** (in a different form) by Christopher Dewdney reprinted from *Demon Pond* (1994) with permission of the author and McClelland & Stewart Inc. **Vigilance** by Christopher Dewdney reprinted from *Alter Sublime* (1980, House of Anansi) with permission of the author. **Summer Cloud** by Roo Borson reprinted from *Water Memory* (1996) with permission of the author and McClelland & Stewart Inc. **The Ecstasy of Skeptics** and **Nakunaru** by Steven Heighton reprinted from *The Ecstasy of Skeptics* (1994, House of Anansi) with permission from the author and the publisher. **Resurrection** by Barbara Gowdy excerpted from *Falling Angels* (1989, Somerville House [Cdn.], Soho Press [U.S.}, Flamingo/HarperCollins [U.K.]) with permission of the author and publishers. Excerpt from **The Small Matter Of Getting There** (1994, Gutter Press) by Christine Slater reprinted with permission of the author and publisher. **Thinking** by Paul Dutton first appeared in *Rampike*. **Bark** by Paul Dutton was previously issued on *Decisive Moments*, a CD by CCMC (Track & Light Records). **Weekend Indians** by Lea Harper previously appeared in *This Magazine*. **Pearl** by Lynn Crosbie reprinted from *Pearl* (1996, House of Anansi) with permission from the author and the publisher. **What's So Easy About 17?** by David Donnell reprinted from *China Blues* (1992) with permission from the author and McClelland & Stewart Inc.

Artwork

1993 poster   Designed by Matthew Remski and Stan Bevington. Letters from Alphacollage by Ludwig Zeller. Used by permission of the artist.

1994 poster   Designed by Death Waits.

1995 poster   Designed by Darren Wershler-Henry and damian lopes.

Other titles from Insomniac Press:

Beneath the Beauty
by Phlip Arima

Beneath the Beauty is Phlip Arima's first collection of poetry. His work is gritty and rhythmic, passionate and uncompromising.

His writing reveals themes like love, life on the street and addiction. Arima has a terrifying clarity of vision in his portrayal of contemporary life. Despite the cruelties inflicted and endured by his characters, he is able to find a compassionate element even in the bleakest of circumstances.

Arima has a similar aesthetic to Charles Bukowski, but there is a sense of hope and dark romanticism throughout his work. Phlip Arima is a powerful poet and storyteller, and his writing is not for the faint of heart.

5 1/4" x 8 1/4" • 80 pages • trade paperback • isbn 1-895837-36-7 • $11.99

What Passes for Love
by Stan Rogal

What Passes for Love is a collection of short stories which shows the dynamics of male-female relationships. These ten short stories by Stan Rogal resonate with many aspects of the mating rituals of men and women: paranoia, obsession, voyeurism, and assimilation.

Stan Rogal's first collection of stories, *What Passes for Love*, is an intriguing search through many relationships, and the emotional turmoil within them. Stan's writing reflects the honesty and unsentimentality, previously seen in his two books of poetry and published stories. Throughout *What Passes for Love* are paintings by Kirsten Johnson.

5 1/4" x 8 1/4" • 144 pages • trade paperback •isbn 1-895837-34-0 • $14.99

Bootlegging Apples on the Road to Redemption
by Mary Elizabeth Grace

This is Grace's first collection of poetry. It is an exploration of the collective self, about all of us trying to find peace; this is a collection of poetry about searching for the truth of one's story and how it is never heard or told, only experienced. It is the second story: our attempts with words to express the sounds and images of the soul. Her writing is soulful, intricate and lyrical. The book comes with a companion CD of music/poetry compositions which are included in the book.

5 1/4" x 8 1/4" • 80 pages • trade paperback with cd • isbn 1-895837-30-8 • $21.99

The Last Word: an insomniac anthology of canadian poetry
edited by michael holmes

The Last Word is a snapshot of the next generation of Canadian poets, the poets who will be taught in schools — voices reflecting the '90s and a new type of writing sensibility. The anthology brings together 51 poets from across Canada, reaching into different regional, ethnic, sexual and social groups. This varied and volatile collection pushes the notion of an anthology to its limits, like a startling Polaroid. Proceeds from the sale of

The Last Word will go to Frontier College, in support of literacy programs across Canada.

5 1/4" x 8 1/4" • 168 pages • trade paperback • isbn 1-895837-32-4 • $16.99

Desire High Heels Red Wine
Timothy Archer, Sky Gilbert, Sonja Mills and Margaret Webb
Sweet, seductive, dark and illegal; this is *Desire, High Heels, Red Wine*, a collection by four gay and lesbian writers. The writing ranges from the abrasive comedy of Sonja Mills to the lyrical and insightful poetry of Margaret Webb, from the campy dialogue of Sky Gilbert to the finely crafted short stories of Timothy Archer. Their writings depict dark, abrasive places populated by bitch divas, leather-clad bodies, and an intuitive sense of sexuality and gender. The writers' works are brought together in an elaborate and striking design by three young designers.

5 1/4" x 8 1/4" • 96 pages • trade paperback • isbn 1-895837-26-X • $12.99

Beds & Shotguns
Diana Fitzgerald Bryden, Paul Howell McCafferty, Tricia Postle and Death Waits
Beds & Shotguns is a metaphor for the extremes of love. It is also a collection by four emerging poets who write about the gamut of experiences between these opposites from romantic to obsessive, fantastic to possessive. These poems and stories capture love in its broadest meanings and are set against a dynamic, lyrical landscape.

5 1/4" x 8 1/4" • 96 pages • trade paperback • isbn 1-895837-28-6 • $13.99

Playing in the Asphalt Garden
Phlip Arima, Jill Battson, Tatiana Freire-Lizama and Stan Rogal
This book features new Canadian urban writers, who express the urban experience — not the city of buildings and streets, but as a concentration of human experience, where a rapid and voluminous exchange of ideas, messages, power and beliefs takes place.

5 3/4" x 9" • 128 pages • trade paperback • isbn 1-895837-20-0 • $14.99

Mad Angels and Amphetamines
Nik Beat, Mary Elizabeth Grace, Noah Leznoff and Matthew Remski
A collection by four emerging Canadian writers and three graphic designers. In this book, design is an integral part of the prose and poetry. Each writer collaborated with a designer so that the graphic design is an interpretation of the writer's works. Nik Beat's lyrical and unpretentious poetry; Noah Leznoff's darkly humourous prose and narrative poetic cycles; Mary Elizabeth Grace's Celtic dialogues and mystical images; and Matthew Remski's medieval symbols and surrealistic style of story; this is the mixture of styles that weave together in *Mad Angels and Amphetamines*.

6" x 9" • 96 pages • trade paperback • isbn 1-895837-14-6 • $12.95

Insomniac Press • 378 Delaware Ave. • Toronto, ON, Canada • M6H 2T8
phone: (416) 536-4308 • fax: (416) 588-4198